Bleed into Me

Native Storiers: A Series of American Narratives

Series Editors

Gerald Vizenor

Diane Glancy

BLEED INTO ME

A Book of Stories

Stephen Graham Jones

UNIVERSITY OF NEBRASKA PRESS   LINCOLN AND LONDON

Publication of this volume
was assisted by
The Virginia Faulkner Fund,
established in memory of
Virginia Faulkner,
editor in chief of the
University of Nebraska Press.

Acknowledgments for the use
of previously published material
appear on pages 147–48
and constitute an extension
of the copyright page.

Library of Congress
Cataloging-in-Publication Data

Jones, Stephen Graham, 1972–
Bleed into me: a book of stories/
Stephen Graham Jones.
    p.   cm.—
(Native stories:
a series of American narratives)
ISBN 0-8032-2605-5
(cloth: alk. paper)
ISBN 0-8032-0516-3
(electronic)
1. Indians of North America
—Fiction
2. United States
—Social life and customs
—Fiction
I. Title
II. Native Stories
ps3560.05395b58 2005
813.6 —dc22
2004020657

Designed and set in Myriad by R. W. Boeche.

ISBN 978-0-8032-4350-7
(paper: alk. paper)

for Brenda, for everything

and for LP

Contents

Columbus landed in the second grade for me, and my teacher made me swallow the names of the boats one by one until in the bathtub of my summer vacation I opened my mouth and they came back out—Niña, Pinta, Santa María—and bobbed on the surface of the water like toys. I clapped my hand over my mouth once, Indian style, then looked up, for my mother, so she could pull the plug, stop all this, but when I opened my mouth again it was just blood and blood and blood.

Overheard in group,
December 12, 1998

Halloween

My father only smoked cigarettes on Independence Day. It was a ritual with him. He would walk all the way to the store, come back with the carton he'd never finish in his armpit, then stand in the road, his capillaries dilated in anticipation, the three of us watching from the porch, waiting, our legs dangling, lips blue from holding our breath all day. We were six and nine and twelve, and it took him forever to light that first cigarette, standing in the road, one hand held up, palm out, like a rodeo rider for his first, long drag, then rotating from the nicotine until the old tattoo on his knuckles was turned to us, upside down, and then, without ever lowering his arm, he would wave us off the porch, out into the pasture with him, two on one side, one on the other, smoke trailing from his nostrils, bottle rockets exploding before us like we were walking into war.

Each of our first cigarettes were cigarettes he let us hold when we ran out of fireworks and just sat there watching all the rest, and it was best that way, because when our eyes watered we could turn our heads up for a delicate bloom of red or green, pretend we were men. But if he ever rounded the corner of the trailer, walked up on one of us squatted down against the fairing out of the wind, our lungs full of smoke—

What we didn't know was that he was training us even then to be little versions of himself. To have discipline. Observe the proper American holidays. But it wasn't easy. Our mother would watch from the window and then not watch, and then kick the cigarette butts deeper under the trailer when we were gone. Because someone had to.

We never tucked our shirts in like she wanted, though, like everybody wanted. We were going to be like him. Everything but the tattoo—*1979*, one number per knuckle, New Year's night twelve years ago. It was the only time our father would drink anymore.

The same store that sold him the cigarettes sold him the beer.

Our mother would hide the keys, and the gun, and only leave the glasses out that she didn't care about anymore, that didn't match anything. That she could sacrifice.

We never heard the countdown to the new year until we were older, either, and by then it was too late. He was still leading whatever part of us is important out into the pasture, his face wet with tears and sometimes blood, and when we got deep enough into the scrub he would send one of us back for the gun, and that was the worst part, because we always knew where it was. Our mother would tell us to be careful but we couldn't look at her, and if you broke down and ran to her and held onto her, tried to tell her—

But that never happened. Each time we waded back out, holding the gun horizontal above our heads with both arms like a soldier in a movie, and then we would learn to shoot by holding the copper bead as low on the butane tank as we could, so that by the time the slug came all the way across the pasture it would pass *under* the tank but not too far under, because if it hit the concrete pad and ricocheted up into the belly, it would be the same: the tank would become a mushroom of heat, taking the trailer with it. Mom.

Each of our first drinks of beer were out there with him, in the wash of relief that came after the four shots he made us take, and it was so good we would hold onto the can with both hands when he tried to take it back, and he would smile, stare down at us—his sons—and it would be like the Fourth of July again, bottle rockets caught in the sheen of our eyes, our ears ringing. Him watching. We were men.

The rest of the night we shot his empty cans the trees held for us, and we woke deaf, our remaining senses heightened to pick up our father breathing on the couch, our mother sleeping to her clock radio, ourselves in six or ten or twelve years, drinking beer whenever we wanted, even if we hated the taste.

Our father was a man of observances. He would only smoke cigarettes on the Fourth of July, only drink beer on New Year's. His monster mask, though. He wore his monster mask every day of the year.

Venison

The first time Sid lied to the state police there was still shaving cream in the creases of his hands from shaving his father's head. The shaving cream caught the cruiser's dummy light in a way that left Sid unable to look the trooper in the face. It had been his first time with a razor. He was twelve. There was no blood at all.

His slick-bald father was watching him from the gate, rubbing his head in some desperate code, looking like someone other than himself.

In the driveway around Sid and the trooper, it was the trooper's cruiser, a primered-grey wrecker, Uncle Trill's girlfriend's truck, and Sid's father's supercab, still new off the lot. The wrecker and Uncle Trill's girlfriend's truck were strung together, blocking all of them in. The wrecker driver had his pregnant wife in the passenger seat, and they were nine months past words already. From the porch Sid's blonde stepmom narrated this chapter of the ongoing tragedy of her life and smoked cigarettes with her left hand. Everything bathed in blue and red, everything balanced on Sid, on how the tail of his father's new supercab fit the nose of his uncle's girlfriend's.

Without sound was one of the answers he didn't give. He also didn't tell the trooper what the trooper already knew: that Trill had come in from offshore specifically for venison, anything but fish or frozen lasagna. That they'd surprised the deer in a bunch just off the road their first day out, three of them still in velvet, then when Trill came back from seeing his girlfriend, Tan, he had her truck, some Bicycle cards from the grocery store; a watermelon. The watermelon was to keep the flies off the deer. The deer were something to shoot besides each other. But they were already bleeding out, as dead as they were going to get. All that was left by dusk was the Bicycle cards, hand after hand of nothing-wild five-card draw, everyone folding out except Trill and Sid's dad, who were in a marathon with each other, a grudge match. Couldn't stop. It happened every time Trill came home. What was at stake was who wore the other's basketball shoes to school in the sixth grade when it had been raining for the whole month; who spit in the peanut butter; who wound up marrying Eileen the first time; who really broke the lamp; who really sold Sid's grandmother's turquoise earrings. Typical brother stuff. Sid understood in a vague, only-child way. It was his first time to see Trill in nearly a year, though. Trill who had named him— *Sidney*—to make him strong like Johnny Cash, then shortened it to Sid, an act of kindness.

So it was about debt, that was one way to understand it, what happened.

Everyone's clothes were already bloody, too.

"Call," Sid's father said, wholly without lips or larynx or any of that, and pushed out six more quarters, his whole stack.

Trill fanned his cards underhand, like the movies. There was enough beer in him that it coated his eyes yellow, but still, his expression wasn't giving anything away. It was drawing things in, though—one thing at least: Sid, crossing the room behind his father, trying hard not to see the cards or let them reflect off the shine of his pupils.

A bluff. His father was bluffing.

And Sid didn't think his eyes widened or his breath sucked in or his fist clenched or his walk got that mechanical, but still, when the hand was over and Sid's father was sitting alone at the table, quarterless, ambushed, transparent, the Glass Man, Trill expertly snapped a beercap out into the watermelon darkness off the back porch and nodded thanks to Sid, he owed him one, and Sid nodded once as if it had been nothing. They stood on the porch listening to the flies until Trill decided he had enough in him that he might could talk his way though the front door of Tan's house, back into what was left of her good graces after taking her truck this afternoon, just to get cigarettes.

"Then go," Sid's father said without looking up from the shuffling cards, but Trill pawed around for a ride instead, because Tan's insurance didn't cover him, either drunk or sober, and he'd made promises to her that he wasn't going to be in town long enough for her to forget.

Sid's father looked up at him finally, through the screen door, across the two years that separated them. "Get in then," he said, already walking to his truck, and Sid sat in the tension between his uncle and his father, exactly in the middle. As they drove, Trill told them of an even better hand he'd played during the heavy weather from three months back, for *real* money, with *real* players, and Sid's father listened and stared straight ahead, locking Trill out of window control. He said he just wanted to keep the new smell in longer.

Trill shook his head and laughed through his nose some because nothing had changed. He even managed to whistle disbelief after a couple of minutes, then four mile markers later forgot he hadn't rolled the window down, tried to spit. Sid cringed. The spit backed down the glass, past the felt weather-stripping, and into the virgin door. Sid's father let the truck coast to a stop, keeping both hands at ten and two, knuckles facing forward, the bridge of his nose brutally pinched.

"Get out," he said, which is how Trill wound up back in Tan's truck, breaking his promises to her, Sid's father leading him home, the deer piled in the bed behind Sid because they were going to be an excuse of some kind, if anybody asked.

Sid's father touched his brake lights twice and Trill flashed his brights to prove he was still awake, and they stepped up onto the blacktop for the second time.

Alone with Sid in the cab, Sid's father collected himself, asked Sid how he thought Trill had been able to take that hand. The only real sound was the radials; the truck was that new. Sid shrugged.

"Only a dollar and a half," he said. "Right?"

Sid's father looked at Sid long enough that Sid looked to the road, to see if they were going to hit something. They weren't. There wasn't anything to hit.

"Mister Trillian James Pease," Sid's father finally said, using his whole mouth this time. "Mister always-comes-out-on-top Trill."

Sid looked hard at the radio dials. He had two dollars in his own pocket. "Here," he said, and laid them face up on the seat by his father's leg.

His father smiled, looking from the bills to Sid, and then nodded yes, like he was seeing it all in perspective after a lifetime of looking too close—that it didn't matter who sold the earrings, but what they *bought* with the money—but then he called Sid by his full name, said hold on, and stood on the power brakes, the new discs locking in place, the new rubber clinging to the asphalt, the venison in back shifting, weighing them down.

For a moment Tan's headlights filled all the mirrors at once, and then the two trucks touched soundlessly in Sid's memory.

His father didn't say anything as he extracted Trill from the three deer.

The first payment hadn't even been made yet.

Minutes later he drove them home—to their own home, the bathroom, where Sid stood over his kneeling father and shaved what the headliner had left of his hair when he'd locked his arms on the steering wheel, closed his eyes for impact. Grief is a hairless thing, Sid's father told him to calm his hands down, and Sid had heard *guilt, complicity,* the delayed shatter of glass. The reflection of his father, rubbing his head in the cruiser's dummy light, his fingers tracing intricate paths across the suddenly pale skin, telling Sid in not so many words that pattern-balding isn't matrilineal like the television says, but passed down from father to son. Strong enough to forgo women altogether. Unavoidable.

Soon enough the current chapter of the ongoing tragedy of Sid's stepmom's life wrapped itself up neatly: the wrecker driver's wife slipping into a labor she was already denying;

the trooper escorting them away at low speed, his report on the bench seat beside him, full enough. Leaving Sid and his father alone in the driveway, absolved. But the flies had followed them home. Three quiet days later their maggots would hatch in the deer carcasses and the repo men would make Sid blow them off with a hose before they towed the supercab, and the more hardy of the lot would molt in midair, never touch the ground, go out into the world with no memory at all of venison or watermelon, go out into the world unable even to distinguish between the two.

Captivity Narrative 109)

His name was Aiche, like the letter. And all he ever meant to do that day was drive down to Great Falls and pawn the rifle, fold the ticket in a piece of plastic and hide it in his wallet for a couple of months. But things happen. Arson. Kidnapping. Gunplay. Aiche, stuck behind an early-morning school bus in residential, his truck too tall and too red to try swinging around. So he pulls forward each time the bus does, stops when it stops, watches the mothers bowl their children out into the yard and then stand there after the bus pulls away, their robes held tight to their throats. They stand there until there's nothing else they can do, and then they go in. Aiche nods at them in turn. The third one nods back, waves as she's already turning away. Aiche takes another drink of his coffee, and then another mother waves at him, holding her hand up long at the end, her arm slowing, eyebrows coming down. Aiche resettles his cup on the dash in what could be taken as a wave back, then rubs a smudge off the blue of the rifle by his leg, because he needs to get sixty dollars out of it. Four houses down, another robed woman waves at him, and now Aiche is burrowed down into the tall collar of his coveralls. One corner and six houses later is when it happens, when it starts happening: two children—eight, eleven—rolling off their front porch, aimed for the bus, the girl leading the boy across the two snows built up in their drive, the boy leaving perfect white breaths in the air, then looking up, pulling back at his sister's arm.

They look at the tall red Ford together, then back to the porch, and Aiche looks with them, to the mother, snapping her head away now, to the bus. It's rolling back, crunching through the slush. Aiche lets off his own brake, rolls back too—careful, careful—and the girl, her mitten already lifted for the door handle on that side of the truck, shakes her head like this is a game, like Aiche is playing with her. And then she gets it, the door. The wind fills the cab, sucking the steam from the coffee on the dash. Aiche has one hand on the wheel, the other on the shifter, and before he can do anything the two children are up, in. Looking at him. The straggly black hair. The skin.

"You're not Uncle Jay," the girl says.

Aiche shakes his head no, says it—*H*—and the mistake he makes is that, instead of touching the brake to stop rolling, he touches the gas, to ease back up to where he was. But it's like there's a chain between his truck and the bus, he's been following it for so many blocks now. When it pulls away, he's behind it, trying to look through his sliding back glass at the children's mother, still there.

"You're Indian," the girl says.

Aiche nods, asks her what school they go to.

She smiles—glitter on her lips—shakes her head. "Different ones," she says.

Aiche purses his lips, nods, nods. Drinks more of the coffee than he means to, just idling down the road now, still craning back for the children's mother. When he looks back in front of him, the bus is gone. Left, right, up. Behind him, the children's mother is standing on the porch again, the phone stretched out with her. Aiche closes his eyes and lets the clutch out, for the long roll downhill. Where the bus had to be going. Because this can still work.

"Here?" he says. "This way?"

The girl shrugs.

The boy isn't saying anything. When Aiche isn't shifting, he rests his hand on the scope of the rifle. He's going to tell the pawnshop owner that the scope alone is worth one-fifty. He drinks the coffee until it's gone and still there's no school, just a convenience store, standing up out of the road.

Aiche tells the girl to stay there, starts to close the door, then comes back for the gun. Because the boy's only eight.

He hooks the strap onto his right shoulder and leans into the glass door, gets two honey buns for the children, more coffee for himself, and sets it all on the counter. The clerk surrounds it with his hands, palm down, fingers spread. Aiche looks at them, looks at them, then follows the arms up to the clerk.

The rifle.

Aiche smiles, looks out to the blond heads of the two children, just there over the line of the dash, then turns back to the clerk.

"This isn't what you think," he says.

"And those are your kids," the clerk says. "I know the drill, man. Just take it easy."

"I'm trying to," Aiche says.

He leaves two dollar bills on the counter and gets into the truck again.

The girl flattens her voice out and tells him Aiche isn't his real name. That it's just a letter, that he's probably Horace or Harry or something.

Aiche nods, backs out, nods some more.

"Where's your school?" he asks her.

She takes him there with her index finger. They pull into the parents' lane. Someone in a sports jacket at the double doors of the gym waves at him, Aiche. At the truck. Aiche looks down at the girl.

"Can't you just take him with you?" he says—the boy.

"It's not his school," she says, then shuts the door hard enough that the ice caked on the glass calves off. Aiche ducks away from the clear view the man in the blazer has to have now, pulls down along the curb, into Great Falls. For legal purposes he tells the boy in as many ways as he can that he's not kidnapping him. The boy says he knows, he's been kidnapped once already, by his dad. His voice isn't shaking.

"Your dad?"

"He's in Arizona."

"Did he take you there?"

"No. We went to a hotel and watched cartoons and then called Mom."

"You know your phone number, don't you?"

The boy nods. Aiche smiles, asks the boy how he'd like to just go home today, skip school, take an Indian holiday? The boy shrugs, looks once at Aiche and then away. "The one with the Manimals," he says.

"What?"

"The cartoon."

"Oh."

"They have guns too."

And then the next thing happens. It's like driving into a mirror: Aiche pulls out of the parents' lane, into the school zone stretching two hundred feet in either direction, and coming at him in the road is his own tall red Ford, right down to the grill. Aiche rotates his head, watching the truck slip past.

Uncle Jay.

The only difference in the two trucks is that Uncle Jay has a red light on top of his cab, a power cable running from it into the door, down to the cigarette lighter. A volunteer fireman.

In Aiche's rearview mirror Uncle Jay slides sideways a bit, trying too hard to turn around. Aiche lets off the gas, to wait, but the truck behind him stops, and Uncle Jay steps down to lock the hubs. In his hands is another rifle.

Aiche looks over at the boy.

The boy's staring straight ahead.

Aiche tells him to put his seatbelt on.

"It is," the boy says.

"Good," Aiche says, and then they're driving as fast the roads will let them, Uncle Jay a block behind, finally spinning out in some mother's yard, Aiche already coasting farther downhill, his coffee percolating into the vents of his defroster. The boy tells him he shouldn't say bad words. Aiche agrees, says he's sorry, and then noses the truck behind the double dumpsters of a thrift store, kills it. There's nothing to say, not really. Just Aiche, coming around to open the boy's door, guiding the boy down, leading him by the hand into the store, past the staring clerks and the secondhand lingerie to the back, where he can think. They stand there while he does, and finally he nods, asks the boy if he still knows his phone number. The boy nods. The pay phone is in the hall with the restrooms. Aiche dials the number the boy recites.

"Who are you?" the mother asks.

"He's okay," Aiche says.

"You can't just do this," she says.

"I'm going to leave him . . . " Aiche says, looking around, looking around, until he doesn't know the name of the place. He closes his eyes. ". . . Can't you just tell me where his school is?" he says, and when the mother starts crying he hangs up as gently as he can.

The boy's looking at him.

Aiche smiles.

"She said to buy you something," he says, and they do, a Manimal action figure from a bin—half man, half puma, with a looped string out his back to hold him by, or hang him with, something.

As they're crossing the parking lot, the boy reaches up for Aiche's hand, and then Aiche lights a match to the rag he cleaned the gun with last night, drops the rag in the dumpster. Because Uncle Jay is a fireman.

Four minutes later, they're back up in residential, Aiche out in the street looking for stadium lights, the kind that schools have. The picture of him that makes the paper the next morning is of him doing that, even: standing at the front of the truck, the rifle leaned across the hood, his right eye held close to the scope, his breath held in, so it won't fog up the lens.

Nothing, though. Just Uncle Jay, climbing the road behind them.

Getting back into the cab for the rest of the chase, Aiche looks north, to the reservation, to Browning, still four hours away, ten minutes of that town, five of that ten residential, and, in residential, six stop signs to slide through. At the second stop sign the near collision is a pale yellow house, because they have to make the downhill turn, and at the fourth the near collision is another red truck, Uncle Jay. The locked hubs of Uncle Jay's truck pop like gunfire as he turns wide in the rearview, rooster-tailing through a lawn.

Aiche starts smiling like it hurts.

"What's your name?" he asks the boy, but the boy doesn't answer, and over the next two miles he tells the boy everything he knows—about sneaking into Glacier with his grandfather to hunt, how they just shot an old moose who wouldn't leave them alone; about the time his best friend in junior high stood out in the road by Starr School all day once, trying to get run over, just to go somewhere else; about how his cousin Natt in Seattle only robs places with water guns, because you don't get in as much trouble if you don't have bullets; about how his plan this morning had been simple—to pawn the rifle and pay back the gas money he had to borrow to get to Great Falls in the first place; about how he thought all this land they were driving through maybe used to be Prickly Pear Valley or something, a long time ago. The boy watches the yellow grass whip by, asks if they're going to a motel room like last time, and Aiche looks out the window with him, out to where the grass is still in relation to them, a fixed point.

"You're supposed to be in school today," he says, "right?"

"Indian holiday," the boy says back, quiet.

Aiche smiles his best tragic smile, nods, and takes his right foot off the accelerator, coasting to a stop. Uncle Jay does the same, blocking the road fifty yards closer to Great Falls. Aiche tells the boy who doesn't have a name that he's sorry, and then the wood stock of the gun is in his hand.

The boy asks Aiche if he's going to turn into a wolf now.

Aiche looks at him, looks at him.

"A wolf?" he says, and then sees, gets it: Manimals, Indians.

He shrugs, looks back to Uncle Jay, says maybe, yeah.

Through Uncle Jay's scope—his rifle eased into the crotch of his door and cab—all there can be is an Indian of some kind, a nephew kidnapped at gunpoint. Motion in the cab, for too long, an action figure getting left behind on the dash, and then the door opening, the nephew on the Indian's knees, the Indian holding the rifle barrel up, its butt against hip bone.

They step down as one.

The Indian keeps the rifle well away from his body, the nephew on his other arm. He stares at Jay, says something that doesn't carry, and then sends the nephew walking over, looking back once and getting waved on for it. Whatever the Indian's saying, he says it again, and this time points, back to where a dumpster is billowing black smoke up into the sky. Like that should be enough.

Aiche. That was his whole name, like the letter.

And already, then, he was pulling away in second gear, picking the action figure off the dashboard, looping it over his rearview mirror so that it blocked the highway patrolmen converging behind him, pulling him over for Driving While Indian, more or less, but unable in the end to charge him with anything worth the ride back into town because the rifle he'd carried onto school grounds and then used on a convenience store clerk had no shells the troopers could find, shells they begged and bargained existence for, tried to dig out of ashtrays and door panels and headliners and every other possible place except for the pockets of my school jeans as I walked from one red truck to another, moving between letters, the smoke marking my return, leading me deeper into town than I ever wanted to go.

To Run
Without Falling

We came up out of the streets like we'd slept there all day, the underbellies of delivery vans and police cruisers passing silent, huge, and black through our field of vision. Our joints pounded with it still. When we looked back the sewers were exhaling steam, and it was rising, so we leaned into the night and ran, the slap of our feet filling the empty spaces around us until it all fell behind and we were there again: the handicapped park, its gentle yellow slide arching up nearly as high as the rocket. Josh rolled over the tall fence in stages, leaving part of the skin of his hand in the chain link, and Mike perched on top, pulling me up after him, and Tim was already there somehow, riding the metal duck into oblivion, his forehead kissing the gravel each time he leaned the spring forward, his mother's prayers the only thing keeping him alive.

Another Friday night.

We huddled in the nose of the rocket and passed a joint counterclockwise, and then Tim's bottle, and when Josh couldn't remember if the guy had said to never take more than two or always take at least two, we swallowed three yellow pills each. It was better living through chemicals. It was something at least. We were fourteen. In the silence after the rush, the gravity acceleration of the rocket pushing our faces into the steel floor as we shuddered towards escape velocity, I saw Josh seeing what he always said he saw: the men of the cocktail party retiring to the porch after dinner to pass the needle, the ladies gossiping into the drawing room with their marijuana cigarettes and snifters of vodka. We were the gentlemen. Josh didn't know none of this would last. I saw what I saw even without the chemicals: a kite's-eye view of a boy as he runs across a backyard, melting over fence after fence, whatever it takes to keep the kite aloft. Mike just stared through the bars of the rocket into the unforgiving irises of the great metal duck. He was the oldest of us. When Tim raised his head to track down Mike's line of sight his glass eye stayed behind, gummed to the floor, some second-grader's saliva reactivating long after his bedtime.

We left the eye. Tim didn't care.

"It's all fun and games," Josh said in his adult voice, leading us down the switchback ramp, back to earth, "until Tim's goddamn eye falls out."

He pushed Tim in jest and Tim fell in earnest, took the rest of us with him, end over end.

Later, dawn already a smell, we would become magnetic ghosts of ourselves on a security tape as we floated up one aisle of a convenience store and down another, touching the gauze and the disinfectant with sticky fingers, professionally gauging the distance from pharmaceuticals to the front door, the parking lot, our passenger curled in the backseat. It would be too late for first aid, though, and we would be large and obvious in the convex mirror anyway, gravel still in the cuffs of our pants from here, from the dipping action of the wheel-

chair seesaws we used as catapults, seesaws greased so quiet that we had to make up for it by screaming our presence,
that we existed. Our voices didn't come back to us, but for one
perfect moment Mike ran after his, down the full length of the
balance bar, his arms out like wings. The deserted park was
his, then and maybe forever, but the bar was only twelve feet
long, and there I was at the end of it. He slammed headfirst
into my gut, the vertebrae piling up in the back of his neck.

We rolled through the gravel to the merry-go-round, and
the three of them pushed me on it faster and faster until the
green beans I'd swallowed whole at dinner became the reaching arms of a spiral galaxy, the delicate tips trailing behind,
the rest whipping ponderously ahead, around and around.
It turned me inside out. Tim's chin split like a plum when he
dove to the ground to avoid the pale green plane of vomit,
and when he lay sideways on the special swings, Josh could
move the red cut like a little mouth. We made a puppet show.
We crept to the nose of the rocket to check on Tim's eye, and
it was still there, the grey strands of gum attached to its backside like a mass of optic nerves, and his chin said something to
it none of us could understand.

On the way down—back to earth—Josh looked around as
if just waking and said *my brother*, but then couldn't take it any
further. We knew which direction he'd been going, though:
this was his brother's park. How we'd found it. Just now was the
closest he'd ever come to talking about it to anyone but me.

"I had become as one bored with television," he said then,
louder, correcting himself in deep falsetto, leading us down
the wheelchair ramp a second time, "and was as yet too young

to properly appreciate AM radio, so I entertained myself with various and sundry substances of foreign manufacture."

"Emphasis on the *sundry*," Mike said, flashing the yellow husk of one of the pills on the blunt tip of his tongue, and by the time Josh turned to push him in the chest Mike was already in motion, racing for the swings. We all chased him there, got belly down on them and absolutely flew, the chains slack each time we rose, until Mike lost it and caught his heels on the downswing. It flipped him up, the plastic seat suddenly at his armpits, his eyes cartoon-size, and then he flopped back, hard and awkward. Because Tim's dad was a doctor, he held Mike's head in his lap and pulled the gravel out, and we gave him the last of the bottle then threw it shattering into the monkey bars, where we didn't go anymore. Now we wouldn't go on the swings, either, probably. Maybe.

Somewhere in the city below us a dry-cleaning van and a police cruiser were passing going opposite ways, eyeing each other across the dividing line and nodding acknowledgment, that yes, they always see each other here, now, like this, their headlights only showing where they're about to go, never any farther. "Don't watch too long," Tim said, his hand on my shoulder, and I nodded: soon enough it would be us in the dry-cleaning van, keeping it in second gear, a delivery schedule on the clipboard on the dash, all neat and proper, the starched-stiff uniforms swaying behind us like husks of what we used to be, what we are now.

"Spacesuits," I said, in wonder, a rocket-shaped swath of stars missing behind us, looming black over our shoulders, and then Josh kicked at a moth and his boot went end over end off his foot, and just before it disappeared a bat or a bird

or some flying thing slammed into it beakfirst. They fell together, at the same rate, and then our boots rained down out
of the sky, trying to get some repeat action, but there wasn't
any. Just us, laughing, waiting, holding our breath. Even
Mike, the back of his hair matted with blood. We didn't walk
the same afterwards, would spend thirty minutes in the car
with masking tape even, drawing stripes onto our black socks
so they'd look enough like shoes for the convenience store,
where there was a sign about proper footwear. They wouldn't
have tread, though, so when we had to run we'd spin out instead, taking shelves and shelves of dry goods down with us,
never making it back to the parking lot.

Because the gravel hurt Tim's feet he climbed onto one
of the special swings and said he needed a wheelchair for this
one, and Josh shook his head no, told him not to say that, not
to ever say that. It almost turned into a fight except for me,
throwing myself down the yellow slide in distraction, the second hump releasing me from gravity.

Josh smiled one side of his face in appreciation, seeing
us at forty remembering this maybe, looking fondly up this
hill at ourselves, and he had just locked his elbow to push his
hand deeper into his pocket for a pack of cigarettes when a
pale beam of light felt across the playground, the broken glass
from our bottle glittering. At the top of the beam was a flashlight in a hand, the hand attached to an arm, the arm cradled
around a boy or girl, it was hard to tell. Skinny, though, and
twisted at the hips. Our age.

The father kept the light low enough that we could see
in his other hand the special key, the one he needed because

they couldn't go over the fence, and it had been a bad night for them, whatever was happening. And now there was us.

Josh was our talker, so he stepped forward, the gravel crunching under his socks. He didn't know what to do with his hands though, his shoulders, any of it. He said something like *sorry*, something like *sir*, but from my place at the spooned-out bottom of the slide, it didn't matter: the man—the father— was still trying to place us, imagine that we could exist in the same world as his child. That there were people who threw it all away. Nothing Josh could have said would have helped. We stood still to not show off how we could move like deer when we needed to, flit off into the night on our straight hips, and finally the man turned the flashlight off, showing us how dark it was, and then deliberately locked the gate behind him, and I could see Tim already couldn't wait for the convenience store, getting caught, paying for all this somehow, but that was still hours away, and it was Friday night, so we tried to play some more, pretend nothing had happened. We leaned back far enough in the normal swings that our hair dragged the earth. We rode the wheelchair seesaw in weak imitation of ourselves. Soon enough Mike climbed onto his metal duck and I spiraled up the rocket to wait for morning, for the warm asphalt to embrace me, obliterate me, the traffic pounding up and down the length of my body. Tim was already there somehow, too, watching his glass eye, not yet touching it. We split the last pill, wasting most of the powder, then touched fists like we'd seen them do in the movies, and then watched as Josh materialized behind Mike and the metal duck, pushing him like they were children, like they belonged here or could have, but then harder, like they were who they were, until Josh was crying without sound and Mike's face was red with gravel, the blood from his mouth slinging up after him, trying to get back in.

"Let go," I whispered to him through the bars, "please," but Tim, who always took care of us, wrapped his hand around my wrist in a way I'd never let anybody else see, and I could feel it rising, the certainty that the man with the special key had locked a part of us in here, and Tim in his way knew it too, so we stood together into the cone of the rocket, as high as we could get, plate steel all around, where we couldn't see anything anymore, just Tim's eye at our feet, staring out across the city. No kites, no sirens, just our bones creaking as we grew into the men we never thought we'd be, chasing our children across the slick grass of April, the fences melting out of the way, the neighborhood playground yawning before us too soon, the bright new equipment hulking in its bed of gravel. Last Friday I saw Josh there. With his son, over in the corner, on the purple dinosaur bolted to the car spring. He had one hand on his son, the other on the burnished steel head of the dinosaur as it rocked back and forth, barely moving. I don't know what his son's name is, but I know what Josh was calling him. We pretended not to recognize each other, that our eyes were just painted on, but then on the seesaw with my own son gravity called in its marker, pulled me back to earth too hard, my son almost catapulting up into the blackness of space.

"Do it again," he said when it was over, his hair resettling strand by strand, and I saw what I always see: the automatic door of the convenience store opening for us as we ran, our shirts full of medicine and candy, each of our sons curled in the backseat of the car, waiting for us.

Episode 43: Incest

An image of Laurie, diving out the front door with, in this order, keys, cigarette, nail polish, and coaster. The coaster is to return to Brianne down the road. Brianne who's going to do her nails for her. But not now: Laurie stands in the driveway holding the coffee cup almost level with her collarbone. The coaster's on it like a lid, and she's ashing onto it. The tire on her Buick is flat again, to the ground. She looks across the pasture but can't quite see to last night, when Jim her husband had the car. Jim who doesn't always make the best decisions. This one was a waitress named Charla, who's unmarried enough that there's mesquite growing up through the ruts of her driveway, the thorns of one branch spaced one and a quarter inches apart. That puts two of the black tips into the Buick's tire. And they're all angled towards the morning sun, rising over Charla's place. Meaning they'd lie down for Jim on the way in, just not on the way out. He probably never saw it when Thomas honked him outside for work at six this morning. Laurie tries to call him but he's out of the shop—his turn to get the beer for the day. The liquor store opens at ten. Laurie arcs her nail polish through the open window of the Buick and spins on the ball of her foot, is on the phone inside of a minute. Because it's not her fault, she's going to make Jim pay for it: she calls the local wrecker out. And they don't even turn the ignition over for less than thirty-five dollars. And they're not supposed to change tires, either, but, too, when Johnny Pan the driver rolls up, Laurie's on the hood sunflowering her toes out to dry. Johnny Pan rolls his tongue along his lower lip in something like thought and twirls the four-way down to the bad tire. The hubcap's already gone—a dog dish by the porch for the dog that got run over last month—and he's spun the five lugs off into his hand before Laurie even looks down at him. They don't even make it inside, just go from the hood (which creases) to the ground (which has sugar ants) to the backseat of the car (which just has memories). Laurie blames it on Jim and them blames it on him again, the next time the tire's flat. For three weeks she blames it on him, holding the end of her fingernail file to the valve core, until, between the tips he's having to leave at the diner and the tab he's running at the wrecking yard, Jim starts looking for a way out. Him and the waitress come full circle: he asks her again for that piece of pie in the window, and she licks her lips again, but this time it's just nerves. He goes down to the wrecking yard to settle, get on the monthly plan maybe, and winds up trading Charla to Johnny Pan for half his bill. He tells Johnny Pan what to say, how to say it. It's like at the Dairy Queen, with Brianne (the failed cosmetologist): just ask her for a haircut afterhours, and she's yours. Johnny Pan stomachs up to the bar of the diner and eyes the pecan pie, the pumpkin pie, "and maybe a piece of you," and the world opens up for him. His second time over, he pulls the mesquite up from Charla's road. There's only about three feet of plant on the surface, but the roots go for twice as long as his truck in both directions. He tells Charla it would have been easier to have just gone around, maybe— a whole new road—and she threads his bangs behind his left ear (she's right-handed) and kisses him between the eyes and this is how people start to get married. Over a Dilly Bar Brianne tells Laurie about the wedding and Laurie looks out across the parking lot and already knows, has already parked at the rest stop outside town and backed the negative cable off the battery, waited all day for Johnny Pan to come give her a jump. You're so predictable, Brianne says, blowing a smoke ring, and Laurie nods, nods, her hand not cupping her belly these days, but her uterus. Little Jim—*Slim Jim* for however long junior high lasts for him—is still five months away, but Laurie can already picture the birth, how she'll move somehow from the backseat of the Buick out to the ground, then up onto the hood, where Jim will leave her as he coasts into town with his head out the window, the neck of his beer just touching the lowest part of the steering wheel. He's almost got the tire bill paid off by now, almost bought Charla's ring for Johnny Pan. The rest Johnny Pan will write off when he has to fire up the wrecker to come get the Buick out of whatever ditch Laurie's giving birth in. It'll be Charla who talks her through it, every light in the wrecker directed at them. They'll hold each other at the neck like sisters, and when Little Jim crowns, shoulders his way out, into all this, she'll hold him to her chest for a moment and look across the bench seat to Johnny Pan, and nod like *please*. Fourteen years later, Brianne clutching the base of his skull with her perfect fingernails, her thick legs around the small of his back, Johnny Pan will look up through the headache rack of his wrecker and see Little Jim, and stop for a moment, remember. Little Jim will be with his basketball team then, in the drive-through for the necessary dip-cones of victory. He's thirteen, then. Only two years later, in that same parking lot with a warm beer poured into a plastic coke bottle, he'll look up, flare his eyes a little in recognition, and then run away the first chance he gets.

Nobody Knows This

The boy was down for the week, because it was supposed to be good for him, working with men, working with horses, being outdoors in the summer. His grandfather told him to stay close to the fence when they pushed the cattle through, then to run the gate closed behind them, and the boy did it eight times before lunch, until the sweat was showing through the back of his leather gloves. The night before, his grandmother had called his grandfather *Marcus* and told him he was too old for the sun like this, for the heat, but the old man—Marcus—had just sat at the table spooning his cereal in bite after bite. The boy was ten. He leaned against the wood slats of the corrals with the hired men and ate Fritos in the shade, and threw them to the horses. The horses picked them out of the mud with their lips, nosed the bags for more. The salt of their sweat was dried on their flanks. The boy's grandfather shied them away with his hat and stood, leaning over the fence, counting the cattle by pair with his index and middle fingers. The boy ate his Fritos chip by chip, staring the opposite direction, at all the old trucks and horse trailers rusting into the ground. One of the hired men said "seventy-eight," almost a whisper, and the boy's grandfather looked down at him like he'd lost count, and the man closed his eyes under his hat brim, where the old man couldn't see. He started the count over, then took his glove off to write it in the notebook he kept in his chest pocket. There were seventy-eight. It was almost one o'clock, the sun straight up, the cattle bawling. The boy's grandfather asked him if he was okay, if he needed to go home maybe, and the boy shook his head no, and when his grandfather was turned around for the heifer silhouetted along the fence, too skittish to come all the way in, too young not to, the hired man who'd known how many head there were tipped the boy's cap forward and told him not to worry, he was always like this, the old man. "Well," the boy's grandfather said to the men, about the stray, and they slouched toward their horses, back to work. The boy held his eyes like they did, like he was looking hard at a faraway thing, and it was because of that that he missed the one named Rod's horse stepping through the rusted center-cap of a mired Model A and into the steel wheel. He heard it, though, saw the back part of it come out of the ground, the pitted rim trailing strands of rubber. The horse crumpled over it, Rod rolling away, coming up with his hat pressed hard to his head. The rest of the men snubbed their horses in, wheeled them around. Rod's horse didn't make a sound, just lay there with its nostrils blown wide, one eye frantic. Its foreleg was still in the wheel. The men tied their horses to the uprights of old trailers and the bumpers of old trucks and stood waiting while Rod worked the cinch loose, keeping one hand on the horse's neck. And then the boy's grandfather stepped forward with the lever-action rifle he kept behind the seat of his truck. He walked up to the horse, held the rifle with one hand, and pulled the trigger, and the hired man who'd said seventy-eight looked over at the boy for a moment, then over his head to the cattle. They pushed in one hundred and ten more that afternoon, found them all bunched up at the water. The heat shimmered above them. The boy ran the gate closed sixteen more times, and didn't drink from his thermos anymore. At the end of the day one of the men looped one end of his rope over the neck of Rod's dead horse, the other around his trailer ball, and dragged the horse off so the coyotes wouldn't spook the cattle through the fence that night. Before bed, the boy's grandfather sat at the table and spooned cereal into his mouth and the boy watched him and didn't watch him. He was already calling him *Marcus* in his head.

Four years later they were deer hunting, the boy and his father and his grandfather again. It was another thing that was supposed to be good for him, turn him into what his father had been, which was just a stamp of *his* father, of Marcus. The boy held his gun loose by his thigh, with one hand like they'd told him and told him not to. They walked three abreast, the boy in the middle, his father and grandfather flanking him. He could see their flannel through the trees sometimes. His vest was bright orange, the only thing his mother had been able to win that year. He felt like a light bulb, one you screw into the porch socket at Halloween. It was November. On the drive to the lease his grandfather had sat in the middle so the boy could get all the gates, stand there holding them while his father and grandfather eased through. Once his father had stepped out to show him how to hook the foot of the post back into the wire loop first, then shoulder the top over. The boy had shrugged. He didn't yet know the nature of panic. All he had to do was shoot a deer, then they could get back in the truck and go home. But first they had to even see a deer. Over a baloney and mustard lunch he told his father how his friend Tim did it from a stand, and his father said back to him that Tim probably did do it like that. The boy said it was probably *good* for him, then stood, leaned back into the trees. His father and grandfather followed minutes later. He could hear them, clambering through the crusted snow. He held the gun with both hands because it was easier to go uphill that way—he could swing the gun ahead, for momentum, something to follow. He tied his jacket around his waist, went up, up, and when he finally saw the deer, a spike, they stared at each other, him breathing hard, the deer not breathing at all, and when he raised the gun he said he was sorry, he really was, then fired. The deer swung around, its back legs knocked out from under it, fell, then rose again, bounded off. The boy looked at his gun, at the blood misted on the snow, and then stepped after the deer. He was going sideways now, not up, and holding the gun with both hands still, his ears ringing, his heart finally pounding with the deer, and then he pushed out through the trees into a cleared space. It was all stumps, chainsaw ragged. Out in the middle of them, his deer was standing, just like the foam ones in the window of the store. He raised his gun again, then thought better of it, stepped closer, and then up onto a broad stump. Only he wasn't looking at the stump. It was coated with ice. He fell hard, sideways into a smaller stump, and didn't feel so much as hear his leg break high up in the thigh, almost in the hip. He pressed his face through the snow into the wet dirt beneath and kicked his other leg, didn't start screaming until he saw his grandfather's bundled form break through the trees. He was pushing his white breath before him, his lips set, and he was coming straight for the boy, holding his lever-action rifle loose by his side. The boy was screaming no, no, and then raising his own gun. Between the two of them was a trail of rich blood left by the deer. Somewhere far off, the boy's father fired his rifle, waiting for an answer, and the boy, ten years old again, and not a horse, gave it to him.

Bile

We were in town to see our father die. It was cirrhosis of the liver, all those beers I carried him before I got too old to trust out of his sight, reaching into that second shelf. Raymond was there, with two changes of clothes, one of them a borrowed suit, and then Charline and my three nephews, watching me from around her hips, their hair plastered to their skulls. Thomas couldn't make it, or, he probably could, but like Dad, he was out there somewhere making news himself, getting arrested in a donut shop for lewd behavior or being questioned for attempted vehicular regicide, a stolen bobtail truck idling in front of the house, small flags screwed into the front fenders to confuse the presidential escort. This time Dad was in the paper just because he was in the background of an ATM security tape, always watching it.

They took him in to question him and he said he was waiting for the money to fall out, which Charline said was reasonable enough, right? Right?

I didn't bring a suit. Maybe I'll wear Dad's if we can ever figure out where he was staying. We take turns with it, one of us staying bedside, playing go-between for him and the nurses, who are trying not to get attached, while the other two scour the city hotel by hotel, asking the same question: old Indian guy, short hair, bad skin, one milky eye? Big Plume? By the second day I can pinpoint the exact moment in my question when the clerks stop listening to me, when I become one voice of many, all speaking in unison, asking the same impossible thing. Four of them have engineering books mixed in with the receipts and newspaper, are using the register for scratch paper. One of them is Pima. He listens all the way to *bad skin*, and then is thinking about one of his relatives, lost too, still the same age in his mind as the last time he saw him.

I leave him to it, but as I'm walking out he whispers something through the cage: *liver messiah*.

By the time I turn back, he's in his calculations again.

That night it's my shift, and I tune in some old military sitcom Dad hasn't seen since Nixon. He says it's been waiting out there for him in the roar and hiss of the ionosphere for years, and I pretend to watch it with him but am really watching him the same way he watched that ATM: waiting for something inside to break. The doctors say two weeks, two days, two hours; have I checked him in the last couple of minutes? Still full of the sitcom, I stand in the hall and attract the doctors with a cigarette, look at the tile floor and ask them what about an *Indian* organ donor, and they laugh and trade looks and take the pulse on the inside of my wrist, say if we were on the reservation, maybe, where wrapping your car around a tree is a varsity sport, but not here, no.

The thin, inner wall of my wrist beats against their fingertips, and the next morning it's thrushing in my right ear. Raymond is in the plastic chair beside me, watching Dad. Waiting. Already he's wearing the shoes that go with the slacks and jacket of his borrowed suit. Last night in Dad's military sitcom, when it was down to the last moment where everything could be happy or sad, they used lard to grease the parachute cords, make them unfold properly in whatever foreign climate they were in, and it worked: their silk sails billowed out with air and they floated off into war with biscuits in their mouths, the end of some other joke I never got.

"Nearly dressed?" I ask Raymond, not really wanting an answer, just an excuse to leave, to bum around the nurse station, whisper what the hotel clerk might have said: *liver messiah*. As one, they hush, pretend not to have heard. "What?" I almost say, but don't. One of them I think nods down to the women's bathroom for me, but then the security guard has a hangover, is tethered to the water fountain between the men's door and the women's. I go in mine, stand on a toilet with my ear to the vent, and hear the nurse whispering to someone else, about me, about my father.

The other nurse says not to report it—me, my question— not to get involved, and then flushes in disgust. She sounds older, like she's seen all this before, and doesn't look away from me when I pass in the hall.

Back in the room Dad's asleep and Charline is rewinding the ATM videotape to watch it again, through the concave bottom of one of the cafeteria glasses. It's supposed to reverse the distortion, cancel the fisheye lens, make Dad look normal.

Later that day I'm at a shelter with a photograph of him, the way he used to call himself Middle-Sized Plume when he was drinking, so he could fit in the bottle better, but again, nothing. I eat two biscuits and take a cup of coffee with me, and on the way out one of the men whispers it through his matted beard—*liver messiah*—and then it passes from mouth to mouth with all due reverence until one man in BDUs takes me by the elbow, leads me outside, points eight buildings down the street, two doors over, second hall on the third floor.

My father's room.

The clerk gives me the key, a notched butter knife looped to a Frisbee with rawhide. It works. I enter expecting him to be there sitting on the bed in his underwear and shirt, fumbling in the sheets for a lit cigarette, a phone ringing somewhere down the hall and him tilting his head to it for a moment, then striking a match. When I was twelve and switching seats with him for the police—my belt loop catching on his buckle until we figured it out—that's all he would ever give the officer: his face flared up yellow for a fraction of a second in the match light. The speech he would recite from the darkness, telling how I was driving him home because he couldn't, what was wrong with that?

His face against the sterile hospital sheets is the same yellow now.

In his hotel room there aren't any pictures of us to keepsake or long-lost tribal rattles to sell or pinstriped suits for me to wear, just tissues that crumble when I touch them, beer-can ashtrays balanced on every sill and ledge, and sitting in the middle of all of it I picture Thomas out there somewhere, insulating himself with the same stuff, paper and ash and spit, like a wasp, then burrowing back into it, emerging days later—now—to roll into town in the back of a pickup, walk up to the nurse station and do what none of us can: hold a gun to his head and give Dad an almost-healthy liver, his own.

I laugh quietly, through my nose, and it doesn't happen—Thomas—and I feel enough like shit for even thinking it that I don't tell Raymond and Charline about the room, because then they might think it too, or see me there thinking it. When they ask me where I got the jacket, though, I lie that it was down at the station, the ambulance left it there when Dad collapsed in the cinderblock interrogation room under the weight of all that suspicion. It's warm.

That night one of the nurses invites us to a party she knows about. Raymond, wearing the slacks now too, shakes his head no responsibly, gravely, and I lean down to Dad to say goodbye, a ritual now. For an instant we're cheek to cheek, closer than we've been in years, and then his hand is at the base of my skull and he's telling me he saw Him in the hall tonight, His great white coat trailing behind Him, and I ask him Who? and he says I know already, but He's flying out in the morning, and the whole time his jaundiced fingers are dancing over the back of my head, as if programming me.

As we're leaving, Charline tilts her head back to hold the fake smile on her face and pretends to be a good sport, saying she'll drink one for him, and we ride with the nurse to one house then another, stand on the lawn for maybe thirty seconds before going in, so Laurence, her oldest, can pee in a bush. The steam rises off it. We don't say anything to each other, and finally she laughs nervously, wades to the door. I follow.

Inside it's chips and beer and two televisions in two different rooms. Two more Indians are on the couch, both guys longhairs, one beer, one water, meaning driver and passenger, and we stare at each other because we don't know what tribe, and then nod at the last possible instant. Standard procedure. You pick it up the first time a white friend leads you across a room just to stand you up by another Indian, arrange you like furniture, like you should have something to say to each other.

Charline's kids disappear into the tires and illegal garden of the backyard, and, now that they're safe, she walks through a dream to the bathroom, to cry the last three days out into someone else's toilet paper. She was the one who took the picture of Dad in bed, then had it developed, so we could show it around. I stand guard at the door, drink the beer that appears in my hand, and talk to a fake-blonde girl who's going to grow up someday to be a model for a blow-up doll. Soon enough someone carries her away under his arm and I'm first in line for the bathroom.

"You okay?" I ask Charline through the hollow core, for the people behind me, and the second time the knuckle of my middle finger knocks on the door it swings away from the contact and Charline is composed again, slimming her shirt down her side. She has makeup on now, angry lips and bruised eyes.

I walk in behind her and just stand there in the white light, finally flush for appearances, follow her to the kitchen. The party's already thinning out. Halfway across town my father is dying. Through the kitchen window Laurence and Theode and Kaney are hiding from each other in barrels of rotted seed. Maybe it was one of them the guys at the shelter were whispering about. Maybe there's some way to die in the backyard no one will ever have known about till now, some way to die that doesn't put stress on the liver. Or leave marks on it anyway.

"What?" Charline says, not looking at them but me, and I turn from her, make the circuit with another beer in hand, come back with the news: our nurse is gone. We don't know how to get back to the hospital, don't have a car to do it in. The two Indian guys are still on the couch, too. We do the nod routine again as I walk through, and this time I hold my cup up in passing, teasing the driver, showing him how easy it would be to take twelve steps backward tonight. Charline asks the hosts if we can use the phone, and when we can, I stretch it out into the backyard to watch my nephews and nieces, tell the hospital operator my father's room number. It takes Raymond a long time to pick up, and when he does the military sitcom is behind him, roaring and hissing.

"He told me," he says, before I can even get started about directions and cabs and how I'll pay him back.

"What?"

"Where it is."

"I was going to tell you."

In the digestive lull that follows I can see him; he's got the jacket part of the suit on now, and he's leaned over on his knees, holding his head in one hand, the phone in the other, talking behind his hair where Dad can't hear him.

"He thought I was Thomas," Raymond goes on. "He said it'll pay for it all."

It's my turn to digest now: we're not talking about the rented room.

"Start over, Ray," and he does, and it's the fisheye movie,

Dad getting money somehow from the ATM machine, or from the people, Raymond's not clear. But he has it. It's tied to the bank of the river in a length of innertube, knotted at both ends like intestines you cook, a brick pulling it down.

Enough to pay for It. To pay Him.

"Ray," I say, "I don't know," and he doesn't either, or can't say it over a landline, and we leave it at that for now, and after he hangs up I hear someone breathing on the phone, on my end or his I don't know. The old nurse, probably. Not getting involved.

Back inside, it's two in the morning and awkward: the people whose house it is are in the back room playing naked reindeer games, and up front it's just me and Charline and her crashed kids, the two Indian guys of no particular tribe, and about six other people, including the blonde. She's on the end of the couch, to the left of the driver, the water-drinking Indian I'm already calling Fish, rubbing his thigh and saying she's a massage therapist, that she shares an office with a licensed hypnotherapist.

We all lean forward for more.

She rubs a little higher on Fish's thigh and spirits his dangly keys out, and with the AA chip I recognize she hypnotizes the willing, insists that the lights be low or it won't work. We crowd around her in the darkness, let her voice lull us into submission, suggestion. It works on two of the people, either that or they pass out, and the other three drift off to find a newspaper for some reason, leaving just four Indians and one blonde around the coffee table.

The blonde snaps suddenly for what feels like minutes and

in the background, in the hum of the city, I hear it: *liver messiah,*
liver messiah, the water lapping at the innertube. "You know
each other," she says to me and Charline and the two Indian
guys, and like that we do, we always have, and I understand
that AA was court-mandated, part of some bargain, the back
end of some offense, and they see my father through my eyes,
pickled in a hospital bed, inventing Someone to save him. The
blonde leans back into the couch, the keys dangling from her
upheld finger, and we watch them long enough that it push-
es us deeper, deeper, until Fish leans forward, slips his key ring
off her finger. We stare at each other with everything already
said, the blonde nodding off in the silence, reinflating, and in
my peripheral vision Charline and the passenger are doing everything but passing paper cups of spit back and forth.

"I'll watch the kids," I tell her, and she stands shyly, because
I'm her brother, but still, in that way she has with her knees
together. It makes her narrow hips look more feminine. She
doesn't look at me as she leaves, stepping into the wet grass
and fermenting seed of the backyard. The passenger follows
on tiptoes, because waking the kids will ruin this, and then,
as he turns to pull the sliding glass door closed behind him,
runs his middle finger under his nose sweetly, part of his junior high conditioning.

I stand, but Fish has me by the wrist. Which is fine. All in
one motion, I turn, shove him back into the couch. He won't
fight me though, just nods into the backyard. "His damn liver wouldn't last your dad five years," he says, and when I still
don't sit, he adds that his wouldn't either. All I'm hearing is *five*
years, though. Maybe I'd have a suit by then.

To keep my hands busy, I roll the wheel of my lighter for my last cigarette, casting a yellow glare over Fish's face for an instant too long. On the floor Kaney coughs and stands silently from the jacket she's under. It falls away from her and she's no one, everyone, asleep. I guide her back down by her thin shoulders and Fish and me watch her side rise, rise. I offer the cigarette to him and instead of taking it he asks me something: "You're not Him, are you?"

I hold my smoke in, step quietly to the sliding door, turn the floodlight off. "I don't know," I tell him, careful not to catch his eye in the glass, and he tells me I'm not from around here. I tell him no shit, I can't even find the damn hospital to watch my father die.

"Three weeks ago," he says, "this varsity football star takes it wrong in the gut, and it mashes him up inside bad, like he's going to die, and when no one will give him any of the organs he needs, even after they've flown in all the good doctors, bumped him up on all the lists, shown his face on the news and everything, the security guard at the hospital steps out for whatever security guards do outside at three in the morning, and there's a body laid out naked-ass cold on the asphalt, with a magic marker showing where to cut on his stomach. A dotted line, like. Taped to his forehead is his driver's license. He signed in the right place."

That's where the three people were going earlier: to get a newspaper, see if He got another one.

"You know where the IHS is?" I ask Fish, and he nods, translating it into hospital, and I pat the kids before I leave, then shake the blonde, tell her to listen for them. Her eyes roll open when I sit her up, her mouth an O, which is enough like *okay* that I can lie to Charline that she was awake when we left. That I was going to come back for them in Raymond's car. That I was going to find Thomas, tell him to get here if he has to hi-jack a mail truck. That I was going to buy a suit on credit some-where, parachute down to the hospital with a biscuit in my mouth. Maybe the nurse is already there, too, at the hospi-tal—*our* nurse. Maybe her beeper went off with an emergen-cy, my father at the PA, offering stacks of ATM money for one good liver.

I have to stop him, at least see him. Things are different now.

But we're not going there either, anymore.

I turn to Fish, slaloming downhill on low-profile tires, the sloped nose of his car inhaling the miles, and he downshifts, nods over the hood at the river, its surface blurry in the light rain, as if just forming. For us. It was him on the phone, breath-ing, listening.

The innertube is right where Dad said, like a piece of in-testine from something too big to wrap my mind around. We remove it cleanly, put it in the backseat, and the whole time I don't say anything, can't. Finally I just make the cigarette mo-tion to my mouth, mutter something about withdrawal. We glide into a convenience store, and before he can stop me, I have the shiny keys, the six-month chip, am strolling the aisles with a handful of crisp twenty-dollar bills. *Five years,* I keep saying, then return to the car with cold cans of beer for my fa-ther, for Fish, who holds the first in his hand like a relic, then takes the rest without question, one after another, well into the slick roads and shattering glass of the night, and the only thing that still rises hot in my throat from that time is that for a moment I saw Myself passing in the plate-glass window of the convenience store, My coat trailing behind me, a Styrofoam cooler swinging at My thigh, heavy with ice and miracles, the hospital somewhere in the city, around every next corner.

Filius Nervosus

1

Men at forty are above the law; my father carries nunchakus to the grocery store. He says he learned them in Vietnam, before he started carrying a briefcase. He was sixteen in 1975; he's never been out of the country. In his high school yearbook he's often caught with plaid pants, a dubious cigarette in his off hand, real casual. Those pants are in my closet, brown and orange. My father was thinner than me at seventeen, but the pants, I can't help myself sometimes. The flared legs swish against each other, up one aisle of the convenience store, down the next. Against a plaid wall I'm invisible from the waist down. I come home with a Slurpee, and over a dinner of mashed potato sandwiches my father tells me that if I ever have to kill anyone, to do it calmly, because if I do it in anger, then a calm me somewhere down the line will feel remorse. It's the psychology of warfare, he says, tearing, chewing.

I went to the army surplus store the other day, just to look around.

The police watch me.

2

All my mother's stories are permutations of the same tired memory: there she is, a mythical seven years old. Backyard. Birthday party, sometimes hers, sometimes my uncle's. Her father who used to watch all the movies has this great idea for all the kids to write down their wishes on little fortune-cookie strips of paper. They do, brows furrowed, elbows furious. Behind them the older generation drinks helium from balloons and talks with a limited roadrunner vocabulary. But there's enough balloons left where nobody has to share. Each of the cousins ties their strip to a balloon. My grandfather is crying and smoking a cigarette to try and hide it, and then in a swirl of motion and extended fingers the balloons are off, the wishes going heavenward, everyone's eyes primitive white and staring.

This is where my mom gets that thing with her voice that she thinks is irony but is really more of an excuse for the pattern of her life. She'll splash some coffee over the edge of her cup so I won't see her cheeks flush and then say that her little-girl wish was just that she wanted her balloon back.

My father does his chucks in the backyard and she makes grocery lists for him, impossible lists that require remote freezer sections on the wrong side of town. She tried to teach me to dance the hustle the other night but we were both trying to hide that we were drunk and it was all wrong.

I keep my wishes in the ashtray of my father's car, because nobody smokes anymore.

3

Friday my father says his secretary's having a garage sale. I know her address, find the ad in the paper. Big block letters: ABORTION GARAGE SALE. Everything must go. No early birds. We get there at seven o'clock and the cars are already lined up. Mostly feminine cars, my dad notes, putting on his aviation shades.

We approach and conversation dies. A haggle stops midway through and money changes hands prematurely. I pick through old vinyl like I recognize any of the names. I do my eyebrows in subdued surprise at finding whatever record it is I'm pretending to look for. My father works his way in in circles, securing the perimeter first, as is his style. He's brought one of my mother's canvas shopping bags for the occasion. He inserts ashtrays and bookends seemingly at random, decorating some diner or halfway house from his youth. I've got an armful of records. He does his chin like *let's go*, so I follow him to the secretary with the fanny pack who absolutely refuses to smile. She looks in his bag, at my records that are marked twenty-five cents, five for a dollar. My father offers her three crisp one-hundred-dollar bills. She shakes her head, calls him by his first name and says "Not enough."

We return to the tables and racks. In an umbrella bucket I find an imitation katana, carved plastic grip, thirty-inch steel blade. Still though, the center of balance is right. My father's unshaven face breaks into a grin. It costs us five hundred dollars to get out of there.

4

That night we sit in the backyard under the droplight and I watch my father's whetstone make little circles on the blade like he can wash it sharp. Three times my nameless friend has honked out front, three times I've not been able to leave. Inside, my mother is still feeding the Lhasa apso we got her on the way back from the garage sale, four and half pounds of apology. I expect the dog to keel over any moment. Me and my father call it Spaz, try not to notice it the rest of the time.

A week drags on, then another.

My father calls from the office and tells me about wind shear and parachuting from low altitudes into wet climates. He says I might need this information. But I don't even have a war to pretend I was in. I listen, make noises like I'm taking notes in my head but really I'm balancing the katana on the palm of my hand, straight up. It's like a piece of me now. After dinner each night my father and me stroll out to the backyard and he takes week-old cantaloupes from the trunk of his car. He lobs them like a softball at my back, and in a single motion I turn, swing, and the two halves fall to the ground.

It's a beautiful thing.

5

One morning before school I wake to find my mother in her house robe, in the kitchen. She's cooking bacon, all of it. She's crying. She tells me the same old story. My father's already off to work. It's just her and the dog and me, and I'm almost gone too. "Watch this," she says, like it might keep me there. She holds the bacon up at waist level and the dog springs up and takes a neat bite. "Yeah," I say. "No, no, *watch*," she says, then holds the bacon at breast level. The dog takes a neat bite, lands softly. Then she holds it over her head, and because I imagine the dog cocking its four-inch legs and flying right past her—because I imagine it becoming small in the sky, leaving us far behind—I drop my toast, a necessary distraction.

The dog waddles over, wide as it is long, a pufferfish, twin black nostrils blowing.

My mother dabs her eyes with the belt of her robe and tells me to call my father, she needs him to pick something up on the way home from work. I try to explain that he's not even there yet, there's no way, but still I have to dial the numbers and listen to it ring and ring. When she finally turns her back I'm already down at the convenience store in my trench coat, the katana on a rope slung over my shoulder.

I pay full price for my Slurpee because I'm a decent person. But I don't have to.

6

The day my mother sends my father for a seedless yellow-meat out-of-season watermelon we have to pick him up from jail. She says he's had it coming to him for a long time; he doesn't say anything. There are nunchaku impressions on the left side of his face, though, meaning whichever shopper or stockboy he intimidated was right-handed. He taught me to take note of these type of things. He doesn't have the watermelon. They get in a fight about it. We have to stop at the martial arts supply store on the way home, for more chucks. I step out of the car there and keep walking, finally get to the secretary's house. The garage sale remains, the innards of her house smeared all over the lawn. I ask her how she's feeling. She says maybe she shouldn't be talking to me, and I tell her don't worry, it's not a genetic thing, really: I'm not like my dad.

Over egg sandwiches she tells me in raw, clinical terms about the procedure she's had visited upon her, and uses lots of peach-pitting analogies so I can really understand. I ask her where my father was going after work. She cocks her head and says that grocery store over on Magnolia, why?

"No reason," I say, and when I'm hiding behind the dumpster in our alley hours later I don't know who to blame, my mother for sending my father in search of impossible items, or my father for believing an impossible item could possibly smooth everything over.

The grocery store on Magnolia calls two days later to schedule an interview, but I fail the bag-boy questions in ways that cause the assistant manager to leave the door to his office open, where people can see us.

7

My father doesn't speak to us for four days, until his face is almost healed, and then he takes it out on the sapling out back, spinning the chucks deep into the night. He's taken to calling everyone Charlie under his breath, so my mother keeps her distance. By the toolshed now there's a whole truckload of seedless yellow-meat watermelons. Sometimes when I'm standing in the yard looking at the tree he'll still lob one my way, and it'll die, and we'll have that. Spaz licks the rinds clean somehow, his tongue like a horse's, as long as his short body. I hear it and my mother in the early mornings, playing their jump-higher-and-higher game, the dog's landing not so soft anymore. It shakes the whole house. If my father slept more than four hours at a time, it'd wake him. But he's on watch.

When it happens is on Good Friday.

It's after school and I'm standing in the backyard staring at the sapling, trying to establish something, a connection or a communion or just a shared shadow. My mother's talking to my father's secretary on the phone, pretending she's a siding peddler. She doesn't know anything about siding. Yesterday it was bibles and guilt. Since she found my garage sale records under the bed she plays them all the time, the globe light over the linoleum floor like a disco ball, light dancing off stove handles and coffee percolators.

And me, I'm standing there, tense, ready for anything, and then I hear it: something whistling through the air, something heavy, almost to my back. I turn, swing effortlessly, and Spaz falls in two pieces to the ground. The distinct smell of bacon grease. My mother dropping the phone. I stand there in my stiff plaid pants, trying to blend with the foliage, and stand there for hours, until my father comes in the front door and their screaming starts, neither taking the blame for me this time. Nobody wants to be guilty. I've given them that at least, to share. Finally my father's magazine collection comes spilling out the bedroom window, my mother's red fingernails just behind them, withdrawing now, and in the silence I know my father is sitting down somewhere, trying to contain himself, his fists at the sides of his head. But he can't. He appears at the door, the chucks held low and limber at his thigh. He thinks he can get away with anything. The air thickens and warms between us, my father's chucks dancing silent across his back, belly, neck, and shoulders until they blur into perfection. I look through them with my face slack as my unborn brother's—acquiring shorthand through the uterine wall, his room decorated with castoff ashtrays and bookends—and then I bring the katana down cleanly, severing the cord, setting us adrift in the lawn, a father and son in a decaying orbit, circling with knees properly bent until all metaphor breaks down and we have to see each other as we are—naked, bleeding down the back of our faces, fighting for what we think is our lives, what we think our lives should be. What they aren't. This is the art of war. We lean into it together, my mother watching through the frosted glass of the kitchen, touching our refracted images with only the tips of her fingers, as if we might shatter into a thousand pieces. We do anyway.

Last Success

Horse Develkin sat the fence and stared off into nothing. *Kaw Liga*, John Paul called him as he walked by, and then broke into song, his oboe-deep voice driving the cowbirds into flight. They filled the sky over J Bar P. In their absence it was Horse at the driveway's edge and fat John Paul half in the crew cab and John Paul's wife who was afraid of the sun and John Paul's daughter who read the paper to Horse when it came on Sundays. Horse who had been able to read for already twelve of his nineteen years. He liked the way the words came out of her mouth though, or maybe it was just her mouth itself. He would sit and watch her read even-voiced over pages of obituaries and comics until there was no difference, until John Paul found them back by the feed shed or somewhere and gave him a shovel for the buffalo shit. It was practically from the movies: father, daughter, drifter, father on one side, daughter and drifter on the other. Across the strip of road from John Paul's section were the blued lights of the new old drive-in, and they'd all seen the shows for free, knew their roles, their lines.

And because of that it was different.

Horse's role as he knew it now was to wait. It was the handful of days immediately following the crime, when nobody yet knew he was a criminal, soon to be the darling child of the media, adopted by the whole Midwest because the drought made them want so bad to look anywhere else than at themselves. Him the criminal, Horse the criminal. He kept it inside because he needed it, ached for it, the not knowing what would happen, whether John Paul would make him work forever to pay it off, whether the daughter would come to him in the night like she never had, out of some skewed breed of pity. Everything was flat and open before him, rolling steadily away to the bruise-colored foothills.

After John Paul had loaded his wife and daughter into the truck and left him orders what to do he still didn't come down off the fence. One of the seven buffalo bulls lowed deep in its chest. In Horse's pocket was the last few inches of pigging string. Evidence. His crime was that he had coaxed each of the buffalo bulls one by one into the chute, then tied the leather tight around the high points of their scrotums. They hadn't caused any trouble. *Kitten bulls* he'd heard the seller call them once, John Paul's prized breeding stock. J Bar P had a restaurant contract for a minimum of seventy hybrid calves, and, aside from the hole in the fence and the thin-hipped Limousin already heavy as a result, it was only the second day they'd been let in with the nervous light-stepping heifers. In no time now their testicles would be shriveled, the leather expanding and contracting with the dew, and it was during this week that Horse sat and watched.

He could do anything when he found out, John Paul could.

The thing about him was that he'd made five fortunes already, and lost them all in neat succession, like dominoes falling. But each time he'd stayed ahead of them. He was a genius, he always said, smart in a corner. He had hired Horse out of the drugstore at town because Doll behind the counter knew Horse was half Blackfeet, that John Paul had some buffaloes, that it wouldn't look bad at all in the new J-Bar-P brochures, not at all. John Paul had looked Horse up and down and said maybe, maybe. Now Horse wore his hair in stunted rough braids the daughter made. She said it made him look real. He lived in the old house John Paul's parents had pulled there on pine logs seventy-two years ago. Tarpaper windows, packrat insulated. Not a tree in sight. For Horse it was a warm place to pass the Dakota winter, a place worth shoveling buffalo shit that still steamed sweet in the early mornings.

On Christmas they had burned the shit pile and stood wet-footed in the melted snow around it listening to John Paul sing his drunken yuletide. The daughter had come out to the old house afterwards and read Horse a newspaper she had from London somehow, and her mouth, the words coming out all British, was something of a gift in itself.

By the end of the week they knew.

At first John Paul just leaned on the pipe fence of the buffalo trap and shook his head and spat and wiped his lips with the back of his sleeve. Horse there guilty beside him, waiting. He waited all afternoon, breathing in and out. The mother watched through parted curtains; the daughter saddled her palomino gelding then took the saddle off and brushed him down. He snorted, his skin jumping in folds. John Paul mumbled to himself: "Twelve thousand dollars, just like that."

He moved his hand in a butterfly motion that never got above his belt.

Twelve thousand dollars. Buffalo burgers, buffalo sausage, fajitas, steaks, stew.

Finally he went inside to eat. Horse checked the water and oiled the windmill and wandered the barn. The daughter spoke to him out of the darkness of the horse stall.

"Dad. He gets like this."

"Yeah."

The gelding's eyes glowed iris green.

"So, y'know, why'd you do it?"

"You mean the string?"

What else.

Horse pawed the ground.

"He won't make that contract now, I don't guess."

"This doesn't only hurt him, Horse Develkin."

Horse watched her there with the hay dust tynsdaling golden all around.

"I didn't really mean to hurt him."

"You should have maybe thought about that some before-hand. About me, or about mom. She's got eczema, you know. God—god*dam*mit, Horse."

She was sixteen. Horse looked away and when he looked back she was gone, only the gelding there staring. He cupped a hand to it and it shied away.

That night he woke to the tiled white ceiling of the county hospital and the pasty-faced nurse told him he was lucky John Paul hadn't used the business end of the shovel, or he'd be dead for sure. She handed him a piece of pigging string in a Ziploc bag, and said in a hushed voice they were lucky too to have found that. It had been a lucky night all around. She smiled a pearly white smile and when she was gone Horse tried to remember any of it, the night, but it was somewhere else. There was white tape tight around his chest though, and his lips sat wrong against his teeth, the left side of his face heavy and numb, pulling his head down.

Soon there was a gaunt-faced man by his bed, mouth like a wolf or a librarian. He introduced himself as Jim Something from the *Dakota Star*. He was up here for the story about the outdated pharmaceuticals, but then he had heard about the string. Everybody had. He asked could he take a picture of it maybe.

Horse looked from him to it and back.

"Just the string, you mean, right?"

Jim Something smiled.

"Nothing else, hoss."

"Twenty-two dollars."

They settled on eleven-fifty and a coke with a straw, and then Jim Something rolled a latex glove on and arranged the string on the light blue blanket over Horse's stomach and the flashes went on for days it seemed, and when they were over Horse finally stumbled into the bathroom and felt to see was everything okay.

This is the Horse Develkin who didn't scream when he peed: he was born to a liquor-store father and a Blackfeet mother; the mother left when he was thirteen and became for him birthday cards from the reservation, the Indian Preserve as his dad called it, the Petting Zoo. Horse learned to drink beer and whiskey at fourteen, and knew girls two years later in the abundant form of a woman named Rita at the five and dime. Stockroom love, hot and cramped. He didn't write his mother about that. The same year as Rita, his older brother got his death money and drove drunk into a snowdrift and they didn't find him until late spring. He looked just the same. When Horse got his death money two years later he drove drunk into drifted snow too, but the snowplow found him and rode him slow in the cab, back to the living. It still had to clear the roads, though. His dad when he was sad in his coffee would tell Horse stories about how beautiful his mom had been, how he never should have chased her off like he had. It was a tragedy, goats in the street and everything. When Horse got enough money to put a new front end under his car he drove it down into the Dakotas, where he traded it for he'd already forgotten what. Probably something dumb like hot meals for a week, magazines to read, someone nice to look at. It was all a cliché, his life already, a cheap book. He didn't write his mom about that either.

Horse heard about it in the paper first, his crime and the crime that had been done on him: the beating, the string square-knotted around his balls. He was all the time afraid the daughter would appear around the corner and catch him reading. But he couldn't help it, it was him, his name, there in the *Dakota Star*, right below the low-pressure system holding an ocean of water over Texas. Front page already, down at the bottom, "The White Man's Buffalo" in bold black letters. The pertinent excerpt from column B was:

> In the later part of that century James H. Develkin's forefathers were on that starving reservation, specifically, his great-great-maternal grandfather, Grey

Elk, and great-great-grandmother, Walks in the
Trees, as well as their pair of young bucks, Last Success and Standing in Place. (*for more see* 3A)

The rest was about the reader's poll on 2G concerning whether John Paul's actions were justified or not (63% yes, 37% no).
These dead Indians were names Horse had never known. As
he wandered the sterile halls looking for a machine to take the
last of his eleven-fifty, his lips kept mouthing *grey elk walks in
the trees, last success standing in place,* until it became for him
a sentence and he couldn't forget it.

The second way Horse heard about the crimes done on
him was from Jim Something, the reporter from the *Dakota
Star.* He had the story from the daughter now. He said he was
interested in James's welfare.

"Horse. It's Horse."

Jim Something smiled and set a microrecorder on the silvery dinner tray, asked if it was okay. The pertinent excerpt of
the interview here was the part that never made it to the radio:

Dakota Star: Your *tribal* registration, James. (angry sound of
papers shuffling)
Horse: I know I'm Blackfoot, okay?
Dakota Star: Black*feet.* Southern Blackfeet. Piegan, Pikuni, lis-
ten.
Horse: Where's John Paul?
Dakota Star: You've got to remember *some*thing, James.
Horse: What did she say about it? (lots of tense staring noises)
Dakota Star: Her story is that her mom got her out of bed
because of the noise, because of you screaming. Out beside

that place they kept you. We have pictures of the ground. The house too. She says that over dinner her dad, Jonathan *Rutlegers*, kept all the pieces of string by his plate. That he was mad, that he gets like that. And that's all. She says the next thing is running out to you and Jonathan Rutlegers. You were of course unconscious by then. And we have the shovel, don't worry. She said she tried to stop him with the leather string. He already had your . . . your pants down. She was the one who called the ambulance. Her voice is on tape, James. (delicate sound of a smile) It's beautiful. It says, and I quote, Hurry, I think he killed him. I think he killed him. (long pause, for effect) Tell me what *you* remember though, James. Horse.

Horse: What's John Paul saying?

Dakota Star: James, you have four broken ribs and a skull fracture. Not to mention your ball— The close call. You could have easily died.

Horse: Tell me again what she said.

The rest of the interview that did make it to the radio in bits and pieces was about how Horse had tied the seven strings that one day, how yes the buffalo were tame, yes the buffalo was a significant animal in some ways he guessed, no, these were the first he had ever seen, no, he didn't know where his mom was. Try the reservation, maybe his dad would know. Then it all came down to sperm counts, average sperm counts for Native American men of his age group. How a sample was required, for legal counsel. There was the cup, virgin white and cold. When Jim Something was gone, Horse sat with the cup until it became too large and too empty, and in retreat he stared out the window to the north where it was still flat in places, where campfires burned small and angry against the night, just outside the city limits. His mouth moved over and over the sentences grey elk walks in the trees, last success standing in place, *he killed him, I think he killed him.* Her mouth. He filled the cup two times in spite of the pain.

The next morning the campfire people were in the hall, the jobless Indian men who had seen the news through plate glass somewhere and drove to it, Blackfeet and Cree and Menominee and Mashpee, a third of New Mexico. Through the rectangled door-window they were all denim jackets and truck-stop bandannas, their shoulders hunched over. For a while there was only the sound of their boot soles, but then suddenly there was no noise at all, no buzzers, no gurney wheels, nothing. It had all stopped: John Paul stood in the door and filled it side to side, a pair of old jeans over his shoulder, a piece of paper in his hand. There was a lilt in his voice like bourbon.

"Don't it just make your brown eyes blue?" he asked them all.

Horse watched him approach, saw how he didn't watch his back.

The piece of paper was the hospital bill, stamped red and paid. He gave it to Horse: $1,478.34.

Horse stared at the receipt for minutes, counting the dollars. The only breathing was John Paul's rasp. When Horse looked up to John Paul, John Paul nodded once and spit a brown stream into the nurses' flowerpot. Horse nodded his head little enough not to hurt. But enough. John Paul tossed the old jeans onto the foot of the bed. They were starched thick and smelled like the daughter, and then Horse saw her at J Bar P waiting for him, leaning on the porch railing like in a painting over a motel bed. He slipped into the jeans as best he could, taking care of his ribs, then walked the gauntlet of staring black eyes in the hall. He answered their silence by remembering how she looked ironing the early mornings away, framed by her gilt white window, delicate columns of shit steam holding up the sky. He kept a hand on John Paul's shoulder, so he wouldn't fall.

On the way out of town they stopped for a shiny new shovel—because the other was evidence now—and John Paul told Horse that in the paper they'd started in calling him the Pope, John Paul, the Great White Father of all Great White Fathers.

"So what do they call me?" Horse asked.

John Paul laughed out the side window and finally broke into song again, "Werewolves of London." For reasons no one bothered with, it had become the anthem for both sides of the 63/37 split, and it was on every station by request at least five times an hour, a war waged in the static land of radio waves.

When it got to the howling part John Paul had his head out the window and almost ran them off the road altogether.

This is the Horse Develkin who hid from phone calls the next three weeks in the old house, listening to the AM news and watching the Indians settle into the parking lot of the drive-in: he learned that his last name alone meant related to the devil, but when paired with Horse, a name that when unproper carried with it running, really meant the demons of genocide were chasing him across the plains of his ancestors, the plains of America. He learned that the buffalo he'd emasculated were also a symbol, that if allowed to breed they would have been just one more instance of Indian culture as roadside novelty, another menu item for the guilty to stomach. It was only talk, though. He had just done it; emasculation was a word, and words were far from the thing at best. They hadn't had the balls in one hand, the string in the other. And he wasn't running. He walked from wall to wall in the house instead, trying to breathe a full breath. He wrote letters to his mom on the back of bean can wrappers and then burned them in a tin bucket to watch the moths ride the updrafts. At night he heard the ghosts of John Paul's parents chasing things across the wooden floor, their long fingers scrabbling after pennies and beer tops and anything shiny. He watched the reflection of his face in the window become him again, except pale and sunless, like his brother's the day they pulled his car out of the snow and counted how he still had seven hundred dollars and change in his wallet, money that nobody wanted. When it was day again he watched for her to walk by the kitchen window of the big house. All the while the farmland sat fallow and the AM radio crackled, making it feel even more dry. The letters came a dozen at a time and John Paul rubber-banded them on the windowsill. Horse was afraid of being caught reading them, so didn't. And it worked. One day towards the end of the three weeks, the night after John Paul had slept on the porch, his ancient ten gauge stuffed with rock salt, she saddled and unsaddled her gelding three times and finally came out to the house, to Horse. She said she felt sorry for him.

The first thing she told him was that most of the rubber-banded letters were from the same group of women in Florida. Horse wanted to say something but all he could think of was the cup over and over. She read him one, which was a photocopy of a page from a book about Blackfeet legend, but her voice was distracted. She flipped through some more and told him maybe the whole book was there, twenty cents at a time, probably a hundred dollars' worth. After reading him a couple of stories about Napi and about Bloodclot she was on her knees behind him, braiding.

"You know your mom's on TV now," she said, "with all this, I mean."

"She says she named me after that one movie."

"She's so pretty, Horse."

"Thank you."

"Dad's going to sell one of the bulls, you know. They're famous now, stars. A couple of days I think."

She finished the braid and messed it up and started over. Her fingers in his hair. She danced all around the question the sperm count hadn't answered—what it had felt like—talked instead about the hospital, the nurses, the news reports. Horse remembered then that it had been her.

"You saved my life."

She laughed.

"No, Dad says you're tougher than that. He said Indians don't die that easy. That's why we had the Old West, Geronimo, Sitting Bull, all that stuff."

"But I heard that recording of you on the radio, on the phone."

"He said that that stuff about your grandparents is made up, too. He told it to Jim in the first place."

"The reporter?"

She finished the braid and began arranging the letters by zip code. Most of them filled with 3s, over and over. Jim jim jim. When she stood, Horse told her thank you again.

"For what?"

"For reading these to me."

"It's nothing."

"No, really. Thanks."

"Horse."

She said it through her teeth, her cheeks smiling. Horse smiled a little too, and when she was gone and it was night he hid in the closet and read more about Napi and about Blood-clot. When the songs rolled across the pasture from the occupied drive-in he could smell meat roasting, make out dim forms against the fires, crossing back and forth, waiting for something, for him.

The next night was the closest he got to her. John Paul was in town yelling for the reporters about the bull he'd lost to the thieving Indians at the drive-in. It was a thing of no evidence though, or none that anybody wanted to look for anyway. There hadn't even been any gunshots. The feast made the state news too, Indians in tepees stalking and eating buffalo again, the seeds of revolt, the Ghost Dance ninety-some years later. The ratings were through the roof. The mother was glued to the TV. The daughter was brushing her gelding down. Horse approached her and they stood at the door of the barn and watched the movie flicker blue in the distance. She was the first to say anything.

"Which one is it?"

"Can't tell."

And there was the gelding right there. They rode him double and bareback out to just shy of the highway, where they could see a spliced-together *White Buffalo* playing, Charles Bronson thin-lipped and full of anger and love, but mostly anger. They sat the gelding and she watched the movie and Horse watched her there in the extra light, and it was over hours too early.

Two days later, right on schedule, John Paul sold one of the now-historical buffaloes to a Plains Indian museum, who planned on mounting it for exhibit, actual string and all. Eight thousand dollars, after taxes. In an effort to raise the price of the remaining five, John Paul said he was going to make of them an endangered species. Horse was repacking the bearings on the J-Bar-P stock trailer before breakfast when the white *Dakota Star* van coasted in. Jim Something kneeled down and watched Horse clean his hands in the diesel.

"How's them ribs, hoss?"

"Horse," Horse said. "It's Horse."

He didn't look up, either. When John Paul climbed down from the windmill where he'd been watching the Indian women bathe, he leaned on the trailer with Jim Something and discussed business arrangements.

"Well let me see it already."

Jim came back from the van with the longest rifle Horse had ever seen, even longer than a goose gun: octagonal barrel, elevated sights, ancient stock twisted like a tree root.

"Sharpes. The real thing, JP. What they used back when."

"Anybody can buy themselves a fancy-ass gun, though."

Jim smiled and in his pocket had a finger-long Big Fifty cartridge. He slid it in the breech and asked what was there? John Paul looked around at all the nothing that was too close and his anyway, and finally pointed his chin out to the drive-in screen. He held his binoculars towards it and said the first footlight on the east side, barely a dot. Jim smiled and sighted for a long time over the trailer tongue. Horse backed away and stood by the daughter who had come to watch, still in her nightgown, her hair everywhere. When the gun finally spoke, it spoke with a deep authority, and a few seconds later John Paul with the binoculars again to his face said *goddamn*, twice. Jim turned to the daughter, her hands over her mouth, no sleep in her eyes.

"Ma'am."

He tipped his co-op hat to her. She smiled and rushed back inside, holding her nightgown around her legs. Jim told John Paul he guessed he'd get full coverage, pictures of course, maybe a hot meal or two, and John Paul just said it again, god*dam*mit, boy. Jim smiled.

"I'll just sleep in the van, back to north somewhere."

As he was pulling away John Paul yelled to just dust them at first, just dust them, be *careful* for God's sake, he just wanted to *endanger* them, and Jim waved his hat out the window and was gone into the north pasture where the heifers were, opposite the drive-in. Horse stayed in his house for the rest of the day, until the daughter came out and read him a handwritten letter Horse told her looked important. It didn't have an envelope, though. It said over and over in a nervous hand, *Girl I love don't worry about me, I'll be eating berries on the way home.* He'd found the pencil in a tin box in a drawer by the window, sharpened it with his knife. At dusk she rode off on her gelding with supper for Jim Something, pork chops and biscuits and gravy, still warm. Horse waited up until she came back with the dishes a full hour later, and then stood out by the trap until something thumped into the dirt at his feet. In a few seconds he heard the voice of a .30/.30 rolling over from the drive-in. Return fire, hours too late. He could feel it in the ground though, how it could have landed anywhere. He stood there with the sterile buffalo until their sluggish movements told him it was time to go back inside.

In three days it was even in the big city papers: there was a buffalo hunter again in the Dakotas. The front-page picture was a mushroomed slug of the past, a thing leaden and undeniable. John Paul stayed mostly inside, making up things for Horse to do: scrape the stock tank, dig out the feed shed with the virgin shovel. The shots came at regular intervals, maybe four in a day, starting around eleven in the morning. The buffalo stood nosing the grass, their bovine eyes not registering danger. Sometimes Horse would throw sweetcake or dirt clods at them, to keep them moving, but they either didn't feel it or thought it meant feed time again. The daughter made two trips a day out to Jim's camp, in shorts and boots, her legs shaved clean for the saddle. Horse read the trickle of letters himself, the whole book of legends twice over, in duplicate. He helped load a pair of the endangered buffaloes up for the Los Angeles Zoo, twelve thousand dollars altogether, John Paul said, it was worth losing that one.

That one was the lame bull that had finally made the zoo listen. Jim had had to put six into it before it finally staggered to its knees and fell, trying to get through the hole in the fence. Horse finished it with a piece of rebar that took days to grind into a point. Jim took pictures of him doing it, the killing, but the film didn't come out, just two vague bodies blurring into one. To make up for it he got a series of shots of the dead buffalo over the next few days, bloating up in the sun and finally sagging back to the ground, the packed dirt mottled with cowbird shadows.

One night a rented helicopter hovered over the drive-in, standing on its beam of light, getting documentary footage of a camp being pelted with wind and dirt. A rock clanged in the blades but there were no voices across the pasture. The next day the drive-in Indians began their final retreat, and John Paul called Jim Something in and explained the situation: if everything was the same come Wednesday, put the two small bulls down. Maybe he could get something for their hides if there were enough fifty-caliber holes in them. Jim just said he was hungry out there all alone. He said it for the daughter and Horse stood there and looked back and forth from one to the other, couldn't remember what he was supposed to do right then, his role. But it had to be something.

That night he walked out to the drive-in and talked to an old Sioux woman picking all the beer cans out of the asphalt. Her back was bad and she had to push the cans into a pile by the speaker post and then follow it down for them. Horse helped her until there were no more, and standing there with her plastic bag of moonlight she told him she never thought she would eat killed-the-old-way buffalo before she died, it was her little girl dream, real medicine. She asked Horse if he'd had any.

"No."

Horse didn't say his name. *White Buffalo* played on the screen without any sound, without any love and without any anger. From a pouch at her side that looked like a bull scrotum the old woman gave Horse some dried meat crushed with berries, and told him to chew it slow and don't ever forget.

That night Horse ate the bitter meat and read the Florida letters and finally opened his eyes onto turnip holes that dangled green rawhide ropes into other worlds. He followed hand over hand, and was reborn in the dirt of a wounded buffalo. When his people found him, all he could ask was Grey Elk? Walks in Trees? Last Success Standing in Place?

They just smiled and opened the smoke hole on his tepee so he wouldn't cough any more. There was no one there he knew. At night he would sometimes crawl out against the star-flecked darkness and his fingers would be looking again for that turnip-hole home. When he finally found it, it was late morning and the radio had forgotten that werewolves ever roamed the earth. He clicked it off and rubbed his eyes. In the trap he fed the last three buffalo with shaking hands, because as much as he looked away, there was still something green and thin at the outside edge of his vision. This is the Horse Develkin who caught the scent of turnips for a moment and closed his eyes tight.

That night the narrow Limousin went into labor and John Paul was already into his second bottle and singing from deep in his belly. To the east there was lightning and on the weather radio word of tornadoes. Farmers for miles around stood sober and waited to be carried away. The last three buffalo turned their faces into the wind for a nostalgic moment and then closed their eyes. Horse led the mother cow breathing hard into the barn, and she was too scared to hook him away. He whispered into her ear.

"It'll be alright momma, we're here, momma, just hold on now, hold on."

In the barn it was Horse and drunk John Paul and John Paul's singing and by eleven, when the power went out, the daughter too, and even the mom, standing far in the corner and crying for the cow, who could only low in pain and roll her eyes. The daughter circled them with the lighter, all the candles blowing out over and over. By two when the calf should have come more than it had, John Paul held the momma cow's ears closed and said that this was trouble, he'd be sober in thirty minutes. He took his shirt off carefully and went and stood in the cold rain coming down, and in the quiet he left, there was Jim Something in the door, backlit by the electric sky. He was covered in mud, but the gun was clean in its fringed sleeve. He looked at the cow panting on its side and looked at Horse lying there with it in the shit she'd let. He smiled his empty-mouthed smile.

"You want I should finish her?"

He held the gun around the middle. Horse shook his head no. "It's breech I think," he said. "Maybe locked."

"Is it one of them?"

"Half."

"Enough," Jim said, smiling, then went to a corner to dry his camera. He stood the gun by the door. Horse said everything he knew into the momma cow's ear, then stopped, suddenly self-conscious that John Paul's wife was listening. She was gone though, maybe back inside, maybe holed up in the feed shed hiding from the moisture and the birth. The candles blew out one by one and the daughter didn't relight them. They were talking in whispers, Jim and the daughter, and then nothing. Just darkness and cow breathing.

Horse held his hands over his ears when the noise of them started, but in his head it was worse: wet sounds, mouths like they were hungry. He whispered words over and over to drown them out and even sang to himself John Paul's dumb mechanical songs, but still he heard when she made a small sound like no.

Horse stood in the darkness. They were quiet again, just hay crunching, cow pain. He thought of Charles Bronson, thin-lipped, and then he remembered walking the hospital hall, guilty, a traitor, the black eyes staring after him. His hand lighting the candle was steady but already when he was walking to their corner he knew he couldn't talk words. Jim was on top of her and she was half fighting him, half holding on. Jim shook his head and said it: "Get the hell out of here, hoss. No joke."

Horse's first kick caught Jim in the lower side of the back. He dropped the candle into the damp hay with his next kick, which rolled Jim off the daughter. She was holding her mouth to scream but no noise. Her shirt unbuttoned, a breast bone-white in the hay dust. As Horse kicked Jim over and over he remembered for the first time that night, waking to John Paul standing over him with the shovel, unsmiling, whiskey and anger in his eyes, mostly anger. The sweated wood taste of the handle coming down out of the darkness, once, twice, and more, his blind hands trying to fight the string. When it was over, Jim was lying in a balled-up pile by the door, tears and red rain coming down off his new beard. He was screaming mist and it filled the wooden place. He started to say something about a hole the size of a fucking *pie* melon but threw up on his legs instead and couldn't say anything. Horse reached for a bridle on the wall and Jim stumbled off into the night, long gun in tow. John Paul spat in his trail and walked inside.

"Never much liked that son of a bitch."

John Paul knew his part, how to deliver his lines. The wetness steamed off him. He walked soberly to the smoldering hay fire with a bucket of rainwater and killed it. The daughter had her shirt buttoned up wrong and was crying, trying to fix it. John Paul stood over her and didn't say anything, which made her cry more and harder. Horse couldn't look in her corner.

It was already just an hour and a half till dawn. They spent it fighting with the mother cow, John Paul and Horse. John Paul was too fat so Horse had to lie on his side with his arm up in her and try to turn it. It felt like nothing else, like another world in there. He blew green birth out of his mouth and the veins stood out in his neck and still he couldn't get it turned. They gave her some time to do it herself, let it happen, but she was weak and this was her first. When dawn was just a handful of minutes away John Paul finally decided it was her or the calf, goddammit, and the calf was probably already dead anyway.

The mother brought a bowl of sugar water from the house, for the cow, because she maybe thought it was a big kitten or dog, and when she was gone John Paul and Horse drank it and spilled it down their shirtfronts and closed their eyes. John Paul wasn't singing. Horse was holding his side where his ribs were separating again.

"You okay there?" John Paul asked.

Horse looked John Paul in the face and nodded yes, said, "What about her, though?"

John Paul breathed a few times slow and then got the rope out, made a small loop. Horse hooked it to something inside the momma and they doubled it around a smooth post and pulled the dead thing unkicking into the world. John Paul severed the umbilical with the toe of his boot and threw the bleeding cord end over end up into the rafters. The mother cow licked the caul off and it would have been beautiful, brown and front-heavy like the bulls, thick shoulders, short face.

John Paul held its head up by the right ear, ran his hand backwards along its wiry soft hair, making it look bigger than it was. He was nodding to himself, looking to Horse and then back to the calf. Finally something inside him shifted and he started in laughing without smiling.

"I'll be good and damned if this was all for nothing, now."

He walked away and came back with two gallons of

bleach, dragging a half whiskey barrel filled with rainwater, sloshing up his arm. He said he figured he must be some kind of genius.

Horse stood covered in birth and shit and blood. The green umbilical cord was dangling from the rafters, whispering to him as he watched and didn't watch John Paul mix the bleach, cradle the calf into the barrel. The mother was too weak to fight for it anymore. The smell in the air was heat. John Paul closed the calf's eyes with his forearm. The bleach water beaded on his starched shirt and rolled off. When a few minutes had passed, the hair fading stopped just short of white, just shy of the last thing that might bring the whole world to the barn. The mix was too weak, John Paul said. He held the calf body under and pointed to the house with his chin.

"Go tell her to give you that other bottle. The one under the sink."

Horse didn't move. John Paul turned his wide back on him, and his voice was large off the tub water and the empty part of the barn: "This isn't the time for you to go getting all Indian on me, boy."

Horse didn't say anything, couldn't, didn't know what there was to say. He rubbed his eye and turned around. Somewhere out on the highway were the drive-in Indians, going somewhere else, maybe home, maybe just going to keep driving until the blacktop quit. He walked slow through the mud to the back door of the house and the mother handed him the bottle when he asked. Her face was dry and cracked. Horse was almost back to the door of the barn when he heard her, the daughter, coming around the house on her gelding.

She was running hard for the north pasture, her hair floating golden white behind her. Horse held the bleach up for her to see him before she left, but it was pulled from his hand and splashed in the empty spaces behind. The deep report of the Sharpes rolled in what felt like minutes after. Horse stepped forward, and there it was again in the ground, the breath of dust, the slug in the ground, close enough to feel, to ache for, with the sound a long time later. He stood still, watching her, mouthing the words, telling her about the berries he was going to be eating on the way home, and in all the news accounts and legends, when the next slug came, it ricocheted off his shirt, whining back into the past, John Paul's calf rising on broken legs to follow, to grow into Charles Bronson's buffalo, a movie he had watched with her once across the pasture, that he was still watching when the deep report washed over him, over all of them.

Conquistadors

The stands are stands salvaged from some abandoned gym, and the arena is a wide oval of school bus hoods, planted topside-in, and in the daytime the packed dirt bakes into a taut, red skin and the tall grass rustles against the inside of the outfacing hoods and birds hang in the air like kites, just staying in one place, but in the night with the fry bread thick in the air and the place lit up with twenty pairs of headlights, that's when the buffalo come up out of their cave in the foothills and the Indian men from town pull on the dull armor the Spaniards left behind and step down into the arena with a red tablecloth from the pizza place or a maroon headliner from the car their uncle died in and for the crowd they point to the old buffalo bull waiting for them, and the old bull shakes his heavy head back and forth, pawing the ground, and then someone drops a beer bottle from the back of the stands and it's started, the fight, the bull charging the bright cloth, the toreador swiveling his hips, balancing on the soft toes of his beaded moccasins, tufts of the thick brown hair caught in his belt buckle, his wristwatch, his wedding ring, and as the bull passes over and over, huffing steam, pawing the ground, the crowd rains down aluminum cans and smoldering cigarettes and painted porcupine quills, and the man starts blowing the whistle he stole from his seventh-grade basketball coach, and the crowd raises its voice with him, and he finally just throws his bright cloth away, draping it over a headlight, tinting the night air red, and then stands there before the bull in his glinting metal until the bull charges, black horns low, hooves collected under it, pounding, and when the bull hooks the man, the man folds around the shaggy head, still holding his arms out somehow, to the side—no hands—and then, just when it seems the bull is going to pin the man to one of the hoods of the buses he rode twenty years ago, it stops, flings the man away, up, out of the haze of the arena, back to 1804, or 1743, or even the fifteenth century, all the ships just dots on the horizon, or the seventh grade, that breakaway lay-up, and the crowd stands, bringing their hands together slowly at first, then louder, and louder, and the one time a white man showed up in his jeep with his fifty-caliber Sharpes with the octagonal barrel and a pair of boys in back to skin the thing out, he looked up from his crude tripod at the denim shins of two hundred Indian people, staring at him, waiting for him to pull the trigger, and he thinned his lips out and backed away, Sharpes held to the side, and said from the darkness that it didn't make any sense, *it didn't make any sense*, but it did, too, to the man falling from the sky two or three hundred years ago, rolling out of his armor on the way down, trailing it behind him, still blowing his chrome whistle, as if the air from it could soften the impact, allow him to stand from his crater, walk into another world. And maybe it can.

These Are the Names I Know

A Bird

We were eight and nine when you found the bird baby dying, dried up in the sun. I told you all about how the momma would never take it back if she smelled us on it, but since you were older and maybe since there were black ants all crawling in the bird baby's mouth already, we took it with us, in the pocket of my shirt close to my heart, where it could stay warm, and I spit love in its mouth once when you weren't looking, because that's how they eat.

Two days later when the bird baby was living and dying finally in a shoebox under your bed, we were out looking for bugs to crush in the eyedropper and I found that spotted eggshell, cut clean in half by maybe a momma bird's beak working from the outside, maybe from a baby bird's working from inside, maybe together. Either way, you said it was the only one you had ever seen and it had to mean something, had to be more than just a shell; you said it was a sign, finding a bird baby and then its shell like that, and it meant the bird was ours, and because I was a girl you wouldn't listen to anything I said, all you could see was you with this bird, how it would look someday.

So I quit talking then, just like that, that easy, fourteen and a half days nobody heard me say a word, not until I had to sit in the office all day waiting for my mom to get off work to come ask me what was wrong and yell at the principal that I was his fault, that I wasn't like this at home, I never shut up then, always talking. She was lying like always, and when she went out to her car for a cigarette I told the principal she was a liar and then I told him some about the bird baby but not all, just about how me and you had seen it, and he held his finger to his lips when my mom came back smelling like smoke and they sat and listened and when I finally ran out of things to say I started making things up about jobs I would never have and people I would never meet and somewhere in the middle of it all I wound up crying through dinner that night thinking about that bird baby under your bed, the little fingers of a yellow lightbulb feeling down through the pencil holes in the box, the sound of you sleeping in the sky above, waiting for everything like it was all going to come to you so right and so perfect.

A Mouse

One job I never had was at a warehouse full of seed. All the warehouses together went something like fourteen acres of covered concrete, no air conditioning, old brick walls that kept it cool even in the summer, brick walls that had people's names carved into them that went back to 1954 and then some. My name was Ring then and I was an eighteen-year-old boy that even the army didn't want, and the way I carved my sign was by drawing a circle, which was good for a while up there above the phone, at least until Reginald put two eyes and a mouth in the middle and made a face out of me.

He quit before I could get him back right, but not before he told me once after work that he had been married years gone by and had lost his wife to cancer in the bone so deep nobody could get it out, and he was raising his little girl back at his trailer alone now, praying hard every night she wouldn't die the same way, but knowing she would just the same.

All he ever ate too was potted meat and Vienna wieners from the can, and even though I was always hungry back then, I never did share any of his food like he wanted me to, even though he said it'd let me grow a mustache like a real man.

The day before he left is the day I think about the most. Him and me were out in warehouse nine, where we kept the better part of our corn, and we were walking around with big soft blocks of camphor, cutting flakes off here and there and leaving them where we thought they'd best keep the rats out. Sometime maybe around six everybody started leaving; we could hear their trucks and Danny's ratty Harley. Me and Reginald were making our way to the dock door trying to get rid of the last of the camphor in big obvious chunks when somebody shut and locked the door not knowing about us, and we both knew without saying it that we were there for the night.

I didn't think it was all that bad, being clocked in fourteen more hours, and had just started arranging bags of treated pink corn for a bed of sorts when I heard Reginald beating on the door with a shovel at the other end of the warehouse, and it was then I remembered about his little girl—maybe Audrey was her name—and I helped him and we tried every door and even broke the skinny glass window out of two of them, but it was no good.

By the time the sun was all done with leaking in the loose places where the walls met the ceiling I couldn't even be around Reginald anymore. I tried though, for a bit, but every time I said anything to him he started shaking around his mouth, so finally I just went back to my corn bed and was lying there burning matches one by one when I saw, half in, half out of one of my bags, a poisoned dead mouse the size of my thumbnail, its skin pulled tight around the bones, eyes gone, teeth bigger than I ever saw, bigger than they should have been, and I started shaking then like Reginald, not really for his little girl back at his trailer waiting for him to get home, but for Reginald himself, for how he ate his potted meat off the end of the same popsicle stick everyday and then shut that stick up in foil and put it in the refrigerator to keep the cancer germs out.

Tin foil and cold. That was all it took.

He never died.

A Frog

Nighttime and our only child is still never born. We sit. We sit together on the couch, opposite ends, me with my books about history, you with yours. Outside it's the rain dying down finally, yellow headlights sometimes on the backside of the drapes, sometimes not. This night while you're asleep on the couch I'll sit arranging the magnets on the refrigerator until three, and in the morning when you wake you won't be able to read the message I've left in the plasticoated symbols trailing up out of blue Louisiana like Lewis and Clark. I too will have forgotten what I meant to say, but the feeling will remain. And I'll be driving. The Cascades. The Sierras.

This night though. Now. Three sets of headlights ago you lit your last cigarette and now you've forgotten it, and I start to cry down the back of my face about things we should be remembering: a bowl in the garage. The smoke gathers around the only lamp in the room and forces the shadows into a tortured dance. The wall is silent. I open the sliding glass door to breathe the after-rain air and close my eyes, see the mountains and the road climbing them. Going to the Sun Road, like in the paper Montana on the map in the glove compartment somewhere.

"Close the door," you say, the air, the air, and I see your hand has found again its cigarette stub. As you breathe in, the ember glows deep under the crusted ash and I see your face once more, see it all at once, in every way I've known you: as a twelve-year-old with hands full of lice and mites and power; as a boy-man looking across the bench seat of your father's truck at me, the dome light making you soft and pale beautiful; as a voice on the other end of the line promising me how good things are, saying it over and over, pleading it into existence; as a sunglassed stranger standing over an abbreviated plot of ochered earth and rubbing the slacks between your fingers because you only want to be somewhere else, anywhere else, never try again; here. The beer, the bourbon, the ice falling silently on the cream carpet to melt into a world of diaphanous trees.

Oh God.

I don't close the door. I leave it open and feel you behind me. I leave it open until the frogsong comes rolling across the shiny pasture into our childless home. *They're praying*, I whisper, where you can't hear me unless you try. They're praying, their voices all together in some desperate plea for more, more, wanting only to drown once and for all in the warm wetness of the pond, that soft second womb where the flies dance higher and higher.

Your eyes bore into the small of my back, where I can still feel you.

"What're you doing?" you ask.

"The frogs," I say.

"The frogs," you say back.

In some places they rain down out of the sky. People have recorded this.

You laugh through your nose but still I don't close the door. Instead I stand there between two worlds and I wait.

And Five Arrows

This it remains.

Three months after you told my dad I was pregnant and he had given us forty-eight dollars in bottled change and shown us the door. Silver and copper and telephone poles fused together with words. I was twenty-one and you were a year older. We were legal. We were running. We were outside Phoenix Arizona, in the flat of a pasture by some little motel-room cabin that we wound up never paying for, even though it was by the week and we were there for four. It was the closest we came to a honeymoon. My mother had given us a parqueted wooden bowl where we separated the dimes from the nickels from the lint. The sun went down every day.

The last of our gas money had just turned into a red fiberglass bow in your hands, and we were out in the pasture with a handful of arrows testing it out against anything that looked worthy.

After a while I was lying down on that blanket we had, trying to talk to you about names. I was saying them all from my book: Abe, Ainge, Alan, Amon, Ash, and then on into the *B*s. You knew it was going to be a boy, had to be, wouldn't even listen to the girl names, but that was back when you would even talk about it, before we found Seattle and the rain.

I was all the way into the *L*s when you started in talking, talking like you were talking to yourself, like I wasn't even there, talking about us being married, living in a house with a dog and maybe even another kid after this one and some neighbors to have cookouts with, and I lay there and listened and I cried hearing you say those things because they were so right, so perfect, so like everything I ever wanted, and you kept talking and talking and after a while I quit really listening to what you were saying.

Sixteen years later though, I can still hear you. I'm still on that blanket with Abe Ainge Alan Amon Ash six months along in my stomach and never going to die, never. I can still hear you, still see you, still believe you. You're leaned back against the azure sky like a Greek statue, shooting arrows straight up. Three of them are buried nose first about fifteen feet out from the edge of my blanket, and you're talking out loud about what kind of car you might want to drive to your work, what kind of work you might want, and you're telling me you'll buy all watermelon stuff for the kitchen like I've always wanted and now another arrow is in the air going up, up, and I'm here on the blanket waiting and waiting and when the arrow disappears I close my eyes and your voice carries me.

The Fear
of Jumping

Donnell had held another boy's hand once like he would never let go. It was church, revival. He had been a boy too. He thought he was about to start crying from the mouth; the preacher was talking just to him. Donnell stood alone and walked alone past all the pews, past all the people with their heads down, and when the preacher cradled him at the base of the skull and lowered him backwards it was into blood the way he remembered it. It washed over him. *There is no sin,* one severe woman leaned forward and whispered into his ear when he was standing below the pulpit, shaking everyone's hands, and he followed her out the door with his eyes. The towel he was wrapped in was white. He left it there that night, just trailed it behind him, and never went back. He was ten, then. At twelve on the way to the dentist's office his mother looked into the backseat for something and caught him with the knife his father had given him for his birthday. He was cutting little *x*'s into every piece of skin his clothes could hide. So he wouldn't cry in the chair. His mother took the knife into her purse and held his arms while the dentist billowed the sheet out over him. He held his breath waiting for it to fall and never saw the birthday knife again, but there were more. All of the *x*'s lowered themselves into his skin like they were hiding, like they were on his side. When the drill started he made promises, promises, and didn't cry, and when he closed his eyes he was two again, the only two he could remember, and his father was walking through the kitchen fast, the steel toe of his work boot slamming into the pork & bean cans Donnell had been stacking into a pyramid by the refrigerator. Two of the cans left half moons on the refrigerator door; one of them marked his chin. When he got home from the dentist he ate all the beans he could find in the cabinets, but none of them tasted right, and he didn't stack the cans on the counter, and he wasn't two anymore. Later that month he scratched a match across the rough paper of the box—a line—and used the flame to light the firecrackers his friend had lined this one frog's mouth with. His friend's father stood over them after it was done, had been standing there before, too, making them finish this thing they'd started. Because you don't learn not to kill things by not killing things. Donnell cut a tiny *x* on the inside of the back of his hand, then traced it in art class with a razor, rubbed india ink into it. It was his first tattoo; he would get more. He wasn't good at talking, so he would get more. In life science they got to dissect a fetal pig. Donnell held it in his hands and looked at it trying to figure it out and the teacher just gave him a knife. It was his birthday. The knife was so sharp. In basketball the coach held his hand up with the tattoo *x* and Donnell became an example, had to run and run all through practice. When it was over he sat on the bench in the empty gymnasium with the towel draped over his head like the players did on TV and breathed and breathed. Through the glass at the end of the gymnasium, where the parents who just had visitation on weekends stood to watch their estranged children play, was the cafeteria, each long table stacked with chairs so the people could mop at night. The lights there were auxiliary; under them was a woman with a severe face. She was watching Donnell. He left his towel on the bench and on the bus home his hand tried to hold a trombone player's hand and then he wanted just to cover his whole body with x's. Everybody watched him get off the bus. He made himself not run. Three years later he stuck one of his knives through the dashboard of his friend's car and cold air came out, air-conditioned air, and he held his face close to it, closed his eyes, and the police officer who had them stopped wasn't impressed, and his mother who had to drive to the jail for him wasn't impressed, and his friend who had to buy a vinyl repair kit wasn't impressed, but the air had been so cold. He remembered back to it as much as he could. His first girlfriend was Laney and he tried to explain things like the air to her and then didn't try, and at a movie once after she'd left early because of him he kept his hand in his pocket and stared at the girl's bare neck in front of him and remembered it as the place the preacher had held him, and he wanted to hold the girl there too. The guidance counselor of his junior year told him he needed to get laid—just like that, said it—so Donnell did, but then came back and still just sat there, looking at his hands. Nothing was different. He still played basketball but only at home when he was stoned and didn't want to play twenty endless questions with his mother. What stuck with him was that you don't learn not to kill things by not killing things, his friend's father standing above them, his shins misted red. In the news was the sketch of a man who had killed thirteen elementary school girls one at a time, over four years. The night before his eighteenth birthday Donnell dreamed of his own father, standing in the cafeteria just past the gymnasium glass, his arms crossed, and Donnell just watched him, and didn't try to kill himself that day. He did go to the wrong science lab, though. The one with the unborn pigs. The same teacher was there. Donnell stood in the doorway looking at him—the teacher—waiting for something that never happened, and kept never happening. The year after graduation he was living in an apartment with somebody, a girl. At night he slept with his first two toes clamped around her Achilles tendon, just to be sure she was there. Like he was holding on. He ate hot dogs from the convenience store and no beans, and during the daytime when he didn't have a job he would watch his girlfriend's niece play with blocks on the carpet for so long that he would finally have to leave, walk, walk. Sometimes he followed the tracks out of town, across the bridge all the junior high kids smoked cigarettes under and wrote their names on. His name was there somewhere, and below it was just water, and then the preacher was talking again, about the pigs, *driven* into the water, and sometimes he sat on the bridge with his legs hanging and waited for them to rise again, small x's carved all over their bodies. In the produce section of the grocery store one day he saw the man he thought had been his dentist long ago, and looked down, away, at the orange potatoes. But that day the dentist was everywhere. Because Donnell had promised. He held his forearms to the sides of his head like a boxer in a corner and walked home, hugging every wall. His girlfriend's niece was still there. She was five

dollars an hour for them—rent. His girlfriend asked him had
he gotten it, the formula, and he just then remembered, shook
his head no, and they sat there like that, the niece stacking
blocks, the girlfriend staring at him, the TV cranking out pictures of the girl everyone thought was going to be number
fourteen. She was blonde and perfect like a human doll. Donnell could still see his hand the way the coach had held it up,
the little blue *x* edged with red. For the next four hours sitting
there watching the niece stack the blocks higher and higher
he rubbed *x*'s into his forearm with the eraser of a pencil, until
his girlfriend saw and started crying, shaking her head no, and
then the niece was crying and Donnell was standing, gathering his jacket; leaving again. The first place he went was the
grocery store, for the formula, but then he walked along the
tracks instead of back to the apartment. After two blocks he
tasted the formula and it was bitter and dry but he made himself swallow it. And there was a woman following him. He
didn't have to look, he knew. She was whispering about his
promise to the dentist. He kicked his legs forward faster and
faster, like his father, walking like his father, through everything it didn't matter, especially through the kids on the bus
watching him after the trombone player had stood, his great
lungs drawing in all the breath there was, and when he got to
the bridge his shins were misted red. He was rising from the
water again. Standing alone at the other end of the bridge
was the perfect blonde girl. They watched each other watch
each other—she was in some grey school outfit, like maybe
she was already a ghost—and when she reached one arm out
to Donnell, one ivory hand, each of her fingers spread, the

woman behind him rushed into his ear, saying it again, *There is no sin,* and there wasn't. Just a man pulling the startling white hood of his sweatshirt over his head and crossing a narrow bridge, walking directly in the middle, holding his elbows in his hands and his eyes straight ahead. The news said she was twelve but he knew she was ten. It was the way she held her hand out, like she would never let go.

Bleed into Me

And then there was the brother (me) who didn't know what to do at the funeral, so just stood there exactly four paces from his brother's casket, following the pattern in the carpet with the toe of his borrowed black shoe. In the inside pocket of the suit jacket he was wearing was the carnation some uncle or cousin had probably meant to pin to a prom date once, years ago. The last time the suit had been worn.

His brother in the casket was waxy and fixed. There were lines in his hair where the comb had dragged through. They must have had to sit him up for that, one person's hands between his shoulder blades, holding him, the other with the comb always in her hands, never between her teeth.

The brother with his toe in the carpet closed his eyes. His father brushed his hand as he passed, dragging smoke in from the porch, crushing his cigarette into the glass ashtray.

"You okay?" he asked.

And then there was the father who didn't know what to say, or how.

The brother shrugged, watched the smoke from the dying cigarette trail up into the parchment lampshade. On the porch on the way in he had stopped to look back at the waiting hearse, and his hand had followed a post up to a support beam, and then he had followed the lip of the support beam to the door. It was a straight line but for one thing: just before the door there was a fleshy lump in the lip of the beam. The brother kept his hand there, swinging to the left some to let an aunt pass, his hanging tie brushing her shoulder, and when he was alone he pulled his hand down. The fleshy lump was a fishing lure, a soft glow-in-the-dark worm, only some prior mourner had run two stick pins in through the face, longways. The pins had pearly heads, were eyes. He didn't know what he had thought the worm was going to be. He put it back, entered the funeral home, approached the casket then backed off four paces to the side, holding his hands one over the other before him.

Everyone was pretending the small green dumpster tucked into the back of the parking lot was just another dumpster. Everyone was eating donuts and laughing with their whole face. The brother started over with his toe, the carpet.

The day after his brother died he had found in his brother's glove compartment an envelope of photographs of the two of them as children, and it wasn't good. He made himself look at each one, though, until he'd placed the season, the year, their age; the photographer. The glue on the envelope had been used up but the backs of the photographs were still tacky from the album his brother had peeled them from at three in the morning, hunched over in the hall, the front door open so that he could flit away the moment their mother's bedcovers rustled, then hide in the bushes all night guarding the house, his pockets full of silverware and heirlooms and pawn receipts, the open front door locked as if he'd meant to pull it shut behind him, then couldn't afford the sound.

In the car on the way to the funeral home the mother had read aloud every street sign and billboard they passed. "Was that it?" she asked, about the street the funeral home wasn't on, slipping behind them. The mother who didn't recognize her own town anymore. The brother who was still getting used to the borrowed suit had shrugged. He had had the headlights on at first, then pushed the knob back in, off. Then on.

One morning he had found one of his dead brother's cigarettes smoldering into the front porch, and he had picked it up for a last drag then dropped it instead, rolled it underfoot. Another time he caught his brother ducking out over the front mat at daybreak, and the two of them fought hard on the dewed-up lawn with their parents and neighbors watching, and the whole time the dead brother was holding one of their mother's gilt-edged plates, and it never broke, and the brother ran backwards down the street with it glinting in the sunlight, his arms out, nose bleeding around his smile, shoulders lifted in apology. Ten months later his whole face would be bleeding from a skull fracture, and his little brother would hold his head in his lap under a guttering dome light with the broken-open face towards his stomach and say all kinds of things he never knew he had had words for, things like *don't worry, it'll be all right, just let it all out, I'm sorry.*

It would be at the high school parking lot, all the trucks circled around for the headlights, and there would be a senior cornerback from another town sitting on the not-yet-dead brother's chest, an unlikely chunk of asphalt held over his head, ready to bring down for the third time, the time that would push the two of them into legend—how the one on top didn't want to do it, how the one on his back wouldn't say he'd had enough. And wouldn't, and wouldn't. And he would live through that and more, too—every way there was to die in Martin County, like he was looking for them—and still show up at the house at three in the morning, to stand in the dark living room and ask himself *what now?*

Once it was the rosewood desk, tied upside down to the roof of a long-hooded car.

Another time it was the condenser unit for the air conditioner.

Towards the end—when he was more a rumor than a brother—it was the plastic forks and spoons left floating in the dishwater; the long copper wire that ran from the antenna to the television set. The fake jewelry his mother had started leaving out for him, closer and closer to his old room.

When he took the desk, he left the stapler and hole punch and paper clip cup on the carpet exactly as his mother had had them on the desk.

That next night his mother hid the gun from the men of the house. Because they would protect her. Even against him. In his eyes in the photographs you can even see it a little. That he was already sorry for everything he was going to do. That his mother and father and brother weren't supposed to miss the cutlery and the wedding bands and the rest, but the photographs. And nobody said it at the funeral but the brother standing in the borrowed suit knew that he was only there because his dead brother had been bad enough for both of them, taken it on himself, and in thanks he drew the cigarette up from the glass ashtray, trying to breathe the end red again, then pocketed the ashtray too.

And then there was the mother who hadn't seen the envelope of photographs yet, who wasn't yet ready to see them. After the funeral when she wasn't wasn't *wasn't* thinking about her son in the ground in his box with the earth baked hard over it like a shell. But one day the shell cracked open, and her son came back. It was three in the morning all night long; things were disappearing again.

At first it was the new set of steak knives, removed one by one from the wooden block she had long ago super-glued at the proper angle to the countertop. Then it was her hair rollers, and then the extra belt for the vacuum cleaner, and then her husband couldn't find the remote one evening, and she knew. Without being told, she knew.

She said his name when no one was in the room, and then with darkness would rush everyone away from the television, off to bed. Once she sat at her missing desk—the stapler and the Rolodex and the lamp all arranged on the carpet in the arc that made the most sense—but then made herself get up; *live*. Because he needed her. She wanted to breastfeed him again, to hold his head to her like that.

"You okay?" her husband asked, and she nodded yes, yes, her uncurled hair falling over her eyes, then disappeared for hours at a time during the day, haunting the pawnshops as only a mother can, inspecting each can opener and doorstop, looking for her son in their curved reflections, their familiar heft. She found her college typewriter at a junk shop on the industrial side of town, and walked out with it cradled in her arms. The warehouses stood solemn around her, in respect.

At a secondhand clothing store that smelled of mothballs and teeth left to dry overnight she found a strand of her pearls in a shoebox spilling over with plastic earrings and dead watches. They were real, the pearls; she talked the clerk down to a dollar-fifty, then forced ten dollars on him, then just emptied her purse on the counter. But it still wasn't enough: her son wasn't eating the food she left on the kitchen table for him. He was going to starve like that.

The household items she recovered she placed in the living room, the kitchen, the entry hall. It was like going back in time.

After two nights without dinner, her son and husband crept into the kitchen at three in the morning, gorged themselves on the food left there and never talked about it.

When the mother's typewriter disappeared again, she left in its place a new ribbon, and then it was gone as well. She followed it all over town: from the pawnshop on Eighth to the one nestled between all the bail bondsmen on Francis Street, by the tracks. All the pawnshop men were the same, too: leather vests, untended sideburns, faces bisected by vertical bars. And they all remembered her dead son, had all just seen him.

Once, leaving the pawnshop on Francis, she passed the boy who had helped steal her rosewood desk. She cinched her scarf around her chin and followed him and followed him, all the glass of his car still shattered from the weight of the desk on the roof. He wasn't going anywhere, though. Just driving.

At a pay phone she called her husband to ask if he was there, maybe—her dead son—and her husband didn't answer, didn't know what to say. That he was hungry.

That was the night she crouched in the bushes, guarding the house. Her plan was to let him in, then close the door behind him.

He must have seen her though, crept past.

And it wasn't because he didn't love her. She was his *mother*. It was because he couldn't help it. Because he had friends who got out of jail and just drove and drove.

Her husband carried her in the next morning. There were old cigarette butts all around her like ash. After that she couldn't leave the house anymore, but three in the morning was still there for her, for all of them, and she would tie her bathrobe around her waist with the knot that made the most sense and her husband would walk ahead of her through the house, hiding the valuables, rearranging them, and her son who was still wearing the borrowed suit would crouch outside each window to catch what she dropped out—the hair dryers and quilts and baking sheets of their life—and he was still smoking the same cigarette his brother had left, watching the window he was under with one eye, the street with the other.

And then there was the father who would always remember his dead son like this: walking up the sidewalk at five years old in moonboots, each of his footsteps timed perfectly with some roofer's nail gun. It was like he was a giant; the father had been changing the oil then, hidden under their old car.

This was years before he ever had to hold a gun on anybody in the living room and mean it. Years before he had to sit in emergency room after emergency room with his wife, telling his youngest son that he did good, he did fine, there was nothing else he could have done. He was slick with blood, though, the son. Trying to read a magazine.

The first thing the father did after the funeral was get a different job, and then a different job, and then a different one after that. He was a security guard and a customer service operator for a video game company and a parachute packer. But none of them lasted. During the day he filled out applications and watched the sky, to see if people would fall from it or float. After the video game company fired him he bought the game at one of his wife's pawnshops and called customer service with questions that always came down not to *how*, but *why?*

He thought he might like to work at a lube shop. Or a zoo. But then he became a roofer, until the roof collapsed out from under him one day and he fell for a moment into some other family's life. They were in the living room building something complicated but magical from popsicle sticks. The two fathers stood looking at each other, and the lesser turned, walked out.

The reason the roof collapsed was a young boy had been walking up the street, and the father had gunned a nail into the shingles with each step the boy took, until the boy was past and there was a creaking half moon of embedded nail heads before the father's knees.

He fell through and didn't stop falling for days, and when he stood it was into another job, writing fortune cookies. It didn't last. He grew his sideburns out and tried to hire on at a pawnshop, but they could tell right away what stage of grief he was in. To prove them wrong he hung from the steel bars of their windows until the sirens came. One of the fortunes that had gotten him fired was that when a father is walking around the house with his dead son, the wife is the only one who can take him away. It had no rhyme, though, the floor boss said, no *reason*, but that was the whole point.

That afternoon the father found a glass ashtray on his workbench. It had been polished for hours. He appreciated that and sat watching it, the vent hood for the kitchen range pushing all his wife's cooking into the garage. It was almost like eating.

He walked the zoo, looking at the animals.

He walked the backyard, watched his formally dressed son steal his mother's typewriter. They looked at each other across the wild grass, and then the son eased out the gate, slipped down the alley.

Nobody ever got anything out of pawn in this family. They always had to buy everything twice, three times, more. The father smiled to himself: *more*.

He tried getting a job as caretaker at the cemetery, but they could see he was still grieving too, and that he didn't have any references. He stood over his son's grave for hours anyway, tending it with his shadow, no pay. One afternoon he stole everyone else's flowers—real and fake—and placed them at his son's headstone by color, but the next morning they were gone again.

"Something's wrong here," he said to himself.

His oldest son was dead. That was what was wrong.

He dug the old moonboots out of the garage and left them on the grave, but then his wife brought them home next week, from the salvage store. His oldest son rustled when he walked, each pocket of his suit choked with flower petals.

The father wanted a parachute too, like other people had. Or to fall through another roof, into a house he *knew*, a living room not piled with items his wife was remembering from a life they'd never lived: shoe buffers, boxes of fire alarms, mirrors with the backing peeled away so you could see the wall behind them.

One morning he found pictures of his two sons arranged in chronological order on the kitchen table, and then the phone rang, and his remaining son was in jail. He had been riding around with one of his dead brother's old friends; they had been looking for a desk.

On the way home the father asked his son for career advice. His son offered him a cigarette. He took it, smoked with one elbow out the window—the son the same, just with the opposite elbow—and remembered the emergency room that time with all the blood. The way the magazine kept slipping from his son's hands.

He wanted to work at a lube shop because he wanted to be under cars again, to be changing oil again, to see the world as a horizontal stripe again, one his dead son could walk up out of. He was too old, though. And cried too much. They didn't tell him that but he knew.

"You should be a comedian," his remaining son had told him minutes after he had asked for career advice, right before they got to their garage. A comedian. So the father walked down the street away from the lube shop trying to make up a joke. Because the world was a funny place. To prove it, a long car drove by with no windows and a beautiful rosewood desk balanced upside down on its roof, two dim shapes in the front seat, their arms out the window trying to hold the desk down.

The father smiled for the first time in weeks.

And then there was the father who lost his son, he said, already gathering speed after the car, so he got a job as an animal handler, just to feel the chimps' hands laced behind his neck, and the street roared with laughter and he ran through it carrying his dead son in his arms, holding his broken face to his stomach, telling him like his other son had that night in the high school parking lot that it would be all right, he could just bleed into him, he would save it all.

Carbon

And the drugs me and Casey did.

I mean goddamn.

All the usual stuff, yeah, but there was the freon cold in our heads, the aerosol fertilizer staining our faces lawn green, the moonshine shit we drank that time in the dark when we couldn't even tell what color the flame burnt. Blue or yellow, it didn't matter. We were already blind. It was like we were running from one pool of mercury to the next in some old Chinese picture book, nobody chasing us. Only us.

We were skinny too, bone thin. Casey a joke of a girl, only one period in eight months, her eyes black and snake flat in the low times, waiting.

But when we weren't waiting. When we were awake four days straight and our hands shook around our cigarettes and the sun came up and made a day for us, for the two of us. Sometimes she'd look at me and my teeth would be chattering around my sawed-off filter and she'd tilt her head back and laugh a little, breathing out her nose, and I'd know that there was nothing else in the world except for her and me.

Her and me.

A man walks into a bar. This is not a joke. I was there.

A man walks into a bar, nothing under one arm, nothing in the other. Just a need. The skin and bones girl, she can see it in the hollows of his eyes, his need. She has a bottle before her, before everything. It's what she does, the only thing. Him and her and the bottle make three, and they sit there through the morning hours and he smiles when she says she's sleepy. He smiles and comes back from the bathroom with three blue pills in his hand. They swim seedlike through the white contents of the bottle, and when the white is gone the blue remains on the glass neck, the threaded lip, and when she smiles, afraid her heart is going to explode, her teeth are watery blue and he takes her.

Just like that.

By the hand. They walk out of the bar and she wants a bed, a couch, a car, a corner dark enough for the two of them to forget each other, but he just kisses her. He tells her that's not what this blue is about. It's something softer. *Feel it.* Soon they find themselves down where the tall grass meets the sky. They laugh and he tells her all the money he has in the world wouldn't buy them bus fare to Wisconsin even.

"Wisconsin?" she says, "I don't want to go there anyway," and when they wake they're holding hands and he leads her wherever he goes.

It was a waiting time, flat black, then the waiting was over, but we knew it would come again. We were right at the end of what felt like five days, looking over into a dry sixth and a hurting seventh. Casey asked me about the bible.

"What did God make on the fifth day anyway?"

I looked around. We were in a grey-tiled garage with a golden eagle Trans Am and on the back wall a huge black velvet painting, a bleached white tiger caught there somehow. Animals all around us. It was nobody's house we knew. They didn't care if the purple holes under our fingernails dripped blood on the concrete, if we wrote our names on the silvery dash of the Trans Am, if we started the car and let it idle all around us like the sonorous thunder of creation.

"On the fifth day," I said minutes after and too late, but couldn't think of anything except the sixth, tomorrow. We were going dry. This was it, again. Casey knew. When we were both in the car she said she could feel it coming already, the waiting. She looked up at me and her eyes were glossy black and going flat. She said she wished tonight was the last night of all, and I stared until I knew she was serious, until I wasn't afraid.

She held my hand up at dash level for me and the watery blood from under my fingernail traced the lines of my hand. She followed one with her fingernail.

"That's your life line," she said, that last word sculpted from the carbon monoxide staining my vision a sable veldt.

Life

line. And I'm not sure what became of her finger.

Imagine the shadow of a bleached white tiger and lose yourself somewhere in it. Not the shadow, but the looking. It's distance is what it is, the spaces between whatever you are and whatever lack of light there is on the ground, feeling inexorably up one blade of grass and then the next, like a sunrise in negative, developing softly, the smell of chemicals all around, the tail moving slowly back and forth. Watch it and feel it, smell it, and when the tiger leaps silently over the golden-lined hoodbird for you as it must, try if you can to remember those spaces, the distance between you and it, the tiger, how it can never reach you because it's chained down to each velvety blade of savanna grass, and each individual blade must bend before you'll ever feel the hard ivory of its mouth.

Sometimes you can even slip into those spaces, find the door and hide.

Don't be fooled though.

Things have been killing each other long before you were born.

It was the tiger that got us. Its eyes pooled silver and deep, the standing-up hair on its back white, not from birth or breeding but from age, from the weight of eons of light.

It just came through the blue smoke for us and all we could do was smile, it moved so slow.

Yes, Casey was dying.

The story. Her dad wanted to hear it over and over, every night at dinner while she was in the back breathing heavy oxygen in the room where they tell me she grew up alone. He'd point his chicken leg across the table at me (this is the same guy Casey told me felt her up at her eleventh birthday) and I'd swallow and then I'd tell him about her hair, how when I woke in the Trans Am, my shirt wet with whatever I had eaten last, I could still smell the tiger musty and heavy all around.

"I've smelled her myself," Casey's father would say, the tiger, and I'd ignore whatever he was really saying and keep going, getting to her hair but not listening to myself anymore. He knew the story. Instead I'd be half in the dream I'd had every night sleeping on his once-plaid couch, about Casey as a little girl, her hair more red than the strawberry it was now, more alive. In the dream all she did was stand there, looking pretty much the same, her arms by her side. I told myself she was waiting for me, waiting to know what to do.

For her dad her hair was where the story ended. When I got to the part where it was morning and the Trans Am bird was back in the hood, he'd start smiling, and then I'd say it, draw in his mind a picture of how the only way I knew something was wrong was that Casey's almost-red hair looked all wrong strung across her lips, which were pale blue like the middle pages of a phone book. He'd smile and lean across the table and bury his index finger in my chest, and with his chicken breath he'd say she was damn lucky he gave her that red hair, wasn't she?

He was a big man.

Every time I said yes.

But that's not where the story ends. That's only where he quits listening.

At the hospital that morning when I was bringing Casey stolen mints to line her bleeding gums with, she went into some close-eyed sort of seizure thing and they took her down for more tests, all the tests, and they told me before they told her. The results. By bad luck they'd found deep in her bones a thing that was killing her, hollowing her out from the inside.

"But she's okay," I argued. "She just breathed some exhaust."

They shook their heads together no and then said yes: "It *was* the toxic levels of carbon monoxide in her blood (among other toxins) that got us looking, yes—and maybe that was a strange blessing of some sort?—but the fact is that those same tests found the thing that was killing her. We're sorry. At least now she can be . . . treated. More comfortable. You know."

An intern hung around after the big guns were gone. He gave me a cup of Styrofoamed coffee. He told me he didn't really want to be a doctor, and I told him I wished Casey and me had died the night before. He stared. He tried to say something, tried to get me to imagine a world where me and Casey were great white Pacific sharks and this thing couldn't touch us, but I looked at him and made him know that the blind hunger would remain, if nothing else, and that would still kill us. He didn't say anything more, and pretty soon the coffee was gone and I was alone.

After a while I started hanging out in the back bedroom with Casey, hiding from her dad and his football, watching *Jeopardy* and *Love Connection* and holding her head up while she drank, trying to get her to forget what that charcoal stuff in the emergency room tasted like when it was pumped from her stomach. It was a good time. It was like we were a unit of some kind, standing there in our last holdout, against the world. But her eyes. She was waiting. She'd found that she could breathe fast in her oxygen mask and hyperventilate. It only lasted a few seconds, a minute at most, but it was something.

They'd stopped the pain pills some time back, doctor's orders.

But we found ways.

The rain. That's what she said she needed, and so that's what I got her. Out on the lawn with her dad, him naked to the waist and hairy red all over. Out on the lawn with me sitting on the porch with my thumb over the nozzle and the hose water arcing up as high as the roof and falling down on them, no rainbows. An Irish song. When she came over she called me the Opposable Thumb of God and I smiled, and then two nights later we were in an alley talking to a friend about the price of gold, and whether we had any credit left. As always, we were shit out of luck, and as always, we found ourselves hours later floating on something, we didn't care what.

"Am I going to die too?" I asked her, and she showed me her lawn-green teeth and said not if she could help it, no, it's not a catching thing.

"Death?" I asked her, thinking of how my family fell dead like dominoes after my dad left us his illegible note, and she laughed and said what else?

That night we slept in the bathroom of a hardware store with quart cans of paint opened all around us, glue on the walls, and we dreamt of living in the radio songs low on the dial, with a two-car garage, kids, a station wagon, everything, everything normal.

We woke and her hair was stuck to the floor, but it came out without even pulling, and we left it there in remembrance of her, of us.

The bald man in the waiting room is praying and praying hard, so that when I close my eyes I see angels up in heaven singing to God with everything they have, singing until their throats bleed and still they sing, afraid of ever stopping.

I can almost hear them. We all almost can, there in the waiting room, Casey getting bombarded somewhere beyond the lead-lined doors, trying not to scream anymore. We know about radiation now, me and her. In the past three months we've read every last one of her little brother's *Incredible Hulk* comic books. We know what the radiation can do, and what it can't.

The praying man takes my hand in his and looks into my eyes for a long time, asks me who I'm waiting for, is it somebody dear?

I nod.

"The first time you saw her, do you remember that?" and I say that I do, I remember: "She was working on a bottle and I showed her something else. Something in blue."

"When did she find out?" he asks, and I know he's talking about the disease. I look past him hanging on my next word and see a cowboy sitting quiet in the corner, acoustically positioned so that all conversation in the room will funnel towards him and be collected by the large dish of his hat. I know he's listening. It's like I'm talking to him, right to him.

And so I confess. I tell him that in a way *I* told her she was dying, that if anybody's killed her it's me, I'm the killer here, dammit, she never had to know, and then I stand and someone tries to pull me down but I'm mad, getting stronger, walking, following my voice to Him.

"What?" I yell at Him, the Listener with the Cowboy Hat, because I know he's God. *What?* And the next thing I know my sin is an anvil black in my chest and somebody is holding me facedown in the bathroom and I'm crying, and before I leave I've been down on one knee for some time, praying with the praying man, praying for God to go back to Texas and leave me and Casey the hell alone, please, just stay away. Look somewhere else.

Three on a bridge, and the water it is cold, yes, but this isn't a joke either.

The man is pushing the girl in the wheelchair and the disease—dis-*ease* as she calls it—rides for free, taking what it wants here in the land beyond symbiosis. The water below laps hungrily at the support posts. Somewhere far above a silver plane hangs suspended. In the middle is this bridge, and it's moving with the world around and around and it doesn't care.

The man parks the girl where she can see over the rail to where the sun will go down. He spits over the edge and it falls end over end into the water. He watches the spit merge and imagines himself doing this once a day every day, until the water rises and swallows him and takes him away, back to his childhood, so he can start over. Maybe back to when he met her, so he can crawl out that bathroom window and never know what they can be together.

Two people on a bridge, the third in its daily remission. None of them are thinking of jumping. There are much easier ways. They both know them all, weigh them in grams, balance them in the empty parts of spoons.

When they leave this bridge the wheelchair will float by its cushion in the running water and then be gone. Two weeks from now the nurse at the front desk of the Place will call looking for them but they'll be gone, *lost*, her dad will say, *regressed*, some sort of remission, probably dead by now. Four months from now she'll be a side story in a tabloid in the grocery store, and people will say she's a miracle, search for her everywhere; she will have forged an unholy alliance with heroin, one that's a deeper green than radiation, stronger. Forty-seven people will die with needles in their arms, most of them senior citizens. Right now though, they hold hands, him and her.

He tells her he's so sorry about all this, it didn't have to happen, and she says "Who are we to say? I never thought of growing old anyways, you know. People don't last forever."

"Not by theirselves, they don't," he says, acting like he's in a movie too (they both want the happy ending), and pulls her up to hug him. For a moment there's one person on the bridge there in the middle of everything, no shadows, no spaces, nothing between.

A man in a cowboy hat sees them from across town and doesn't cry or smile. He just tells the cab driver to drive, *drive,* man, anywhere.

Time passes, builds up behind us like a dust cloud. I save my nosebleeds in a cup because I'm afraid of the finality of dying. I imagine giving Casey my kidney, my lung, my heart, becoming her, taking her place. Me and her. We lie. We steal. We cheat. Anything to achieve the height we need, to maintain it. We feel guilty for beating a man so we trade for weak cocaine that makes us sick, and we call it justice.

We laugh. All the drugs we did because we were afraid of each other. It's a joke.

Everything.

Like that time we had the freon and our synaptic pathways were so icy slick there was zero resistance for the current of thought and everything was happening in a silent montage, I remember Casey finger-drawing on a table and whispering to me like it was secret that we were the Kite People, that we weren't supposed to ever come down, that we were together up here forever, in the sky-blue clouds with the silver mercury lining, up here where nothing could touch us.

I think it was love.

My noseblood in the cup has been trying to coagulate into a scab lately, and when it finally does I'm going to leave it in a tidepool somewhere (wherever the oceans are), so at least some of me can have another chance.

Tigers should run so fast.

Every Night Was Halloween

Tim

"Tonight," Lyndon said, pointing with one finger over the steering wheel as we crossed the line into America, "tonight," and then we were there—the slick streets of town, the storefronts decorated with ghouls and ghosts and ninety-nine-cent specials. Our eyes glistened with alcohol. We were in town to look for Sheri, like every month, our teeth set, my fingertips drumming into the back of the seat until Dance cupped them under his hand.

He pointed with his chin out my open window and there was Old Amos across the street, backlit by a wall of television sets, his breath messing with the reception.

"Put *him* in a paper bag," Lyndon said, his eyes flashing in the rearview.

We coasted past without saying anything, because Amos would want a ride back to the reservation, was already looking toward it even, wavering, one hand about to start pointing.

"Good sign," Don Ann said from the front seat.

"Amos?" Dance asked. It was Don Ann's first time with us, looking for Sheri.

"That he didn't see us."

"Shit."

"No," Lyndon said, "maybe it is," and then we didn't argue except for Dance, who leaned back into the seat and said to-night again, careful to keep his eyes out his side of the car. If we went slower than twenty miles per hour, the gravel in the centercaps of the wheels rattled, so we went fifteen, because Sheri's got to know that sound. This used to be her car. The night she left, she'd kicked some snow at it, laughed, said it would probably be mine next.

I'd smiled, took the cigarette from her mouth and huddled over it, winter whipping past, pushing us into the van Lyndon was always never fixing up.

"You're really doing it," I said to her, my eyes narrowed to show her it was a question, almost.

She nodded, held the cigarette between two of her gloved fingers. There was ice on the red of her nail polish, through the tear in the tip of her glove. She was four years older than me, Lyndon's big sister. I relit the cigarette for her three times, trying to make her stay, and then on the fourth she twined her fingers into my hair and kissed me hard on the lips, told me to say goodbye for her.

That was eight months ago already. Eight months I'd never told Lyndon how long I stood there against his van that night, watching her ski jacket swirl away, my lips already cold but the base of my skull where she'd touched me hot.

I turned my head away from it, watching town smear by, Don Ann still talking about Amos, how he was the coyote or the raven or something in this story. Dance looked at me for a flash, just being sure he knew I knew how much shit Don Ann was full of, and I shrugged, wanting him to be right, Don Ann. For this time to be different.

The only reason he was along was because his aunt was supposed to have seen her—Sheri—walking past a daycare somewhere in residential, where all the streets were named for trees: Ash, Birch, Dogwood, Fir. Lyndon followed Don Ann's index finger onto Hickory. The daycare was Elm Grove. It was bathed orange with Halloween.

"Trick or treat," Dance said, already rolling out his door, gathering speed for the line of flickering jack-o'-lanterns down the sidewalk, smiling at him.

"Shit," Lyndon said, Dance wading through the sparks, "like we don't look *enough* like Indians already?"

Don Ann was already swiveling for patrol cars. Which left Dance for me: I tackled him into a suburban hay bale. The sparks settled around us, sending up tendrils of smoke.

"Tonight," he said, getting Lyndon's voice perfect like he could, then pushed off, dived back into the car. The toes of his boots were waxy from the votive candles that had flared in the pumpkins' mouths and eyes and triangular noses, then suffocated. By the time we made Oak, he'd tricked a thread from the outer edge of the sole, wound it up through the wax, lit it with a careful match. The three kids at the intersection (surfer, Lone Ranger, alien) appreciated it, made faces like they saw this everyday, so what?

Between the four of us in the car there was twelve feet of hair. It whipped our eyes even at fifteen miles per hour, but we were used to it, squinting ahead. The parents on their spooky porches with their phones in hand watched us rattle past, and we watched them back until we got to a non-tree street with virgin pumpkins.

"No," Lyndon said into the rearview mirror, and Dance just raised his chin to him, innocent. Like if he did anything now it was going to be Lyndon's fault, for bringing it up. Our beer was balanced on a fencepost on the way out of town, in a place where no one's headlights had ever washed.

"Trick or treat," Don Ann mumbled to the next group of eleven-year-old goblins, raising his fingers on the doorsill to them. The rocks in the centercap were singing. In my mind they were polished smooth enough from all these trips into town that we could empty them out into our palms, trade them for gas to get home, melt them into our belt buckles and onto our fingers: a ring for Sheri.

Eight months ago, I didn't smoke. Now I couldn't breathe it in deep enough.

"Look," I said, leaning over the seat, and Lyndon feathered the brakes in a way that we all had to hold our breaths: four houses up was Sheri's competition dress, with the tin-can conchos and the beadwork laid on so heavy that when the rain came in Browning that time, the leather stretched until her hem dragged the ground.

With her were three shorter Indians.

For the length of four residential lots the polished rocks clung respectfully to the inner wall of their centercaps, then fell at once when we pulled alongside, stopping, our hair settling over our shoulders, out the windows, all around.

"Trick or treat," Don Ann said, looking but not looking at her, and two of the three Indians turned, their braids nylon and too black, their legs and arms in pantyhose, their fathers' chamois stretched over their waists, their war paint perfectly symmetrical, probably hypoallergenic.

"Sheri?" Lyndon said, the corners of his mouth twitching with hope, the red of our brake lights massed behind us. I said it too—*Sheri*—and she even turned around, leading with her chin, but it wasn't her, not quite.

I closed my eyes and pushed my knees into the back of Don Ann's seat. When I opened them Lyndon was stalking across the front of the car, holding one hand up harmlessly and touching Sheri's dress with the other—the can bottoms we'd cut out with tin snips until our fingers bled, the leather she bought through the mail when we couldn't figure out how to make any of our deer hides soft for her. It had probably brought twenty-five dollars at the pawnshop, if Sheri told them it was her grandmother's or something. An old Indian trick. We all knew it except Lyndon, who wasn't understanding anything anymore, was too close to her—having to go by touch because he no longer trusted his eyes.

Don Ann had his leg across the front seat holding the brake down, keeping us in place. It couldn't last, though. Lyndon was already shaking his head no, no, and in the moments before he pulled one of the conchos off, tearing the leather, exposing a white hip, salmon-colored panties, one of the Indians with the transparent eyebrows lightly touched the tips of my hair. And I let him. And I touched his too but my fingers were numb and I was thinking about my boots anyway, the ones my father left behind in a cooler on the porch, soaking in transmission fluid to make them waterproof, make them stain all my socks pink.

"*No*," Lyndon said then, out loud, in the way that means *run*, and two blocks later the concho was still in his hand. He was driving with his wrist, curb to curb, the tin cutting into the thin flesh of his palm, and instead of saying anything I fumbled a cigarette alive, but after one drag the cherry arced across the backseat, into Dance's lap, *under* Dance. He stood on his heels and his shoulders, and we were both digging, digging, Lyndon fishtailing in slow motion through Juniper and Oak and Spruce, his head moments ahead of the steering wheel.

We never found it, either, the cherry, or maybe it burned through the rusted floorboard, rose from the asphalt as a flashing red light in every mirror at once.

Lyndon laughed without turning around, keeping both hands firmly on the wheel, Dance's waxy toe easing the .22 pistol out from under the front seat. Don Ann knew what was happening but wouldn't look, wouldn't be a part.

"Tonight," I whispered to him, smiling with my teeth, rubbing my numb fingertips together, and when the officer leaned over the roof with his tin badge and his regulation issue tied down to his thigh, the string whipping in the wind, all it took was one *trick or treat?* and then our .22 was popping somewhere far away, the pantyhose melting from my mouth and Sheri's so that when we kissed, it was real, skin to skin, and her fingers were so hot on the back of my head that I pushed closer to her, closer, told her to stay, she'd never make it to town without a car.

Don Ann

Tim was dressed like his father: the oily boots, the denim jacket, the pants. None of us said anything about it except Dance, and then it was just "nice costume." Tim flipped him off from close range, Lyndon shouldered the case of beer, and then they were balancing it on their fencepost, on the inside of a long curve of highway.

"We should just drink it," I told them.

"You don't have to come," Lyndon said back, so I followed them up to the car. I didn't even remember what she looked like, really—Sheri—just all the prize money she used to bring home from the powwows, all the pictures of her in the paper.

Before we left I'd looked up Elm Grove in the phone book, made myself memorize the address: 2234 West Maple. Like she was just going to be standing there waiting for us. For Lyndon, anyway. He'd believe anything.

"Tonight," he said, and Dance breathed out evenly.

Tim's father had split maybe a week after Sheri did. Usually he waited for the reservation to thaw out some, but then basketball went regional in February and he had to follow bad enough that he just walked out of his clothes, left them on the porch. When the bus came back all hangdog, he wasn't with them. Jimmy Branch said he'd seen him in the stands there, in a stolen windbreaker and jogging pants, and Tim just shrugged, said that was why he didn't play. They were already looking for Sheri every week then, and just finding the same Indians over and over: Amos and Boge and Looks Twice.

"Any of them know where the beer is?" I asked.

Lyndon smiled, made another turn towards Maple. "They're asleep by the time we get there," he said—the drunks he carted home on weekends—and in the vanity mirror Tim nodded absently.

Amos was related to me somehow, too, but then we all were, maybe Dance the most, when he was kicking through the line of pumpkins, the seeds sticking to his pants. He didn't wipe them off, either. Their sticky smell drafted through the car, out the window, back into the night.

"What now?" I asked—now that she hadn't been there—but nobody was talking so we drove on through the forest of residential, the season, *Halloween*, Lyndon stopping to let werewolves and zombies and ballerinas parade through the yellow headlights. The parents didn't thank us.

"What was she wearing?" Lyndon asked me then, and I stared at the dashboard and lied, said my aunt thought it was her elk tooth dress.

"Bullshit?" Dance said. Just that.

I shrugged, lifted my fingers for three of the trick-or-treaters, smearing past. "She didn't see her that good," I told them, trying to get out of it, stall, anything to get us back to the fencepost, but then suddenly I wasn't lying: there she was, a few houses up, just like I'd said. Maybe because I'd said.

Sheri.

The only sound in the car was Dance, his breath rasping in, staying there. His hair was rustling too—his head going *no*—but I didn't remember that until later, after she'd turned to us, whoever she was, or wasn't.

Lyndon never even knew I had to catch the brake for him when he got out. Nobody did except Amos, later, and that was just because I told him.

"What else?" he asked me, his face pitted with age.

By then we were at the fencepost with the beer, all of it, and Dance was breathing hard—one side of him sprayed red—and Lyndon was crying into the loose dirt of the ditch and Tim was still in the car, in the backseat.

"She didn't sound right," I said, about Sheri, "the dress I mean." I couldn't make the tin noise with my mouth though, the rustling sound of her dance.

Amos nodded anyway, cracked another beer open. "How's Joanie?"

"Janey," I corrected. My mother.

"Janey," Amos repeated.

"Same." It was what I always said when people asked, but with Amos I didn't know what it might mean: the same as when?

"Will they catch—*come* after us?" I asked, Dance sweeping the pale seeds from his pants legs finally. They fell like thunder, were going to fill the ditch with orange next summer.

Amos laughed, wiped his nose on the back of his sleeve. "You're Indian," he said, "what do you think?" I told him I wasn't even supposed to have been there with them, that my aunt was just saying she saw her—Sheri—to get people to listen to her.

"Rosalyn," Amos said, nostalgia rising in his throat.

"Racine," I corrected, and he nodded, lifted his beer to her, wherever she was, whoever she was. It glinted. Beyond it there were little moons all up and down the road—the reflectors showing the way we'd come, the way we were going. Six miles back was a grocery store parking lot with a flatbed trailer up on blocks. It had a pyramid of pumpkins on it. In one of the pumpkins near the bottom a .22 pistol was suspended, four spent shells in the cylinder, the grip wiped so clean it was transparent. But still. The cop had radioed our plates into dispatch, had to have. And then there were the three little Indians and the non-Sheri, too.

They'd caught up with us by the time it happened—dissonant tin conchos shimmering into my peripheral vision, three lone feathers standing up from elastic headbands. Like us, they had their lips pursed, their teeth set. Maybe we'd seen the same TV shows, sat by each other in the matinee all the Saturdays of our lives. Their faces went red-then-dark, red-then-dark, the patrol car's light strobing them, giving them shadows then taking them back. The officer hadn't even had to turn the siren on. It was Halloween. We were routine, probably wearing wigs too.

God.

On his hands and knees still, Lyndon threw up again, the long, hot strings connecting his insides to the ground. Amos drew his shoulders together to keep from laughing, was already apologizing about this to Lyndon, to Dance, watching him hard.

I shook my head no to Dance though, please. Let it be over.

"Your ears," Dance said to me, tapping his own like he was deaf, "they still going?"

I nodded, made myself look away, into my hand, the sixth cigarette of my life. They were Tim's. I'd coughed at first but already I was needing more, all of them.

What I didn't tell Amos was that the third little Indian had just stood there when the shooting started, the interior of Lyndon's car bright with death, and in the middle of it all my fingers waved on the doorsill again, and the little Indian's moved in response, over his nylon thigh: goodbye.

Goodbye.

"It's *funny?*" Lyndon asked, suddenly a smell, Dance rising from his station on the fence. I had been smiling, couldn't stop. The beer was warm in my hand. The car was an inky wash of pain. Tim was dead. The girl at the booth of our first gas run had asked us what we were supposed to be tonight, and I'd just said *Indians*, but we'd already filled the tank by then, there was nothing she could do, nothing any of us could.

Lyndon

Already I couldn't hear anything as we pulled away from the curb. The cop's gun, my .22. The drive back through residential wasn't even real: Fir, Dogwood, Birch, Ash. Sheri. A mound of abandoned pumpkins. Don Ann and Dance screaming at each other in the close confines of the car, their voices muted, the dome light flickering.

Sheri. Tim. Halloween.

"*Amos,*" Don Ann finally said in a way I could understand, Famous Amos, standing in front of a camera now, his profile fractured on the bank of television sets, all of them turning to us, the car.

"Amos," I repeated in my inner ear, braking gently, every security camera on the block trained on us, framed in front of the electronics store. Don Ann looked from Tim to the medic Amos had once been and shook his head, leaned into the dash above the glove compartment with the bridge of his nose. It left a dent. I ran my finger over it, tasted it.

"You crawl out of a pumpkin there?" Amos said to Dance, Dance's legs still trailing orange tissue, and I saw the three of us—the four of us, *all* of us—each balled up in a pumpkin back at the grocery store, our heads between our knees, hiding, incubating. But they were too small.

For once, Dance didn't say anything back to Amos, and then Amos was at my window, his breath drawing the water from my eyes at last: "Find her this time, president?"

Sheri.

I shook my head no, panning back and forth across the hood. The can bottom I'd pulled off Sheri's dress was still in my hand; it didn't weigh anything. I was holding it so tight just to keep it from floating away, or because if it did float away—back to Browning or Spokane or New Mexico—I was going with it. To her, Tim standing in the rain watching her dance, shoes in hand. It was just the two of them that day, the old women silhouetted in the entryway of their dry lodges, nodding, looking away.

"Let go," Don Ann said, and then took the can bottom from me, handed it back to Dance.

"Sorry," Dance said, wiping it down, holding it by the edges, whipping it out the window. It never hit the ground.

Amos was already looking down the road for us—behind, ahead. His eyes were slits, like they are in the movies. Because of that I knew we'd make it. But then he was walking across the headlights, his shadow projected against the brick warehouse, crisp and black and Indian, twenty feet tall, and in comparison he was small, slouched, drunk, nodding to Don Ann and calling him *Dalton*. Don Ann didn't correct him.

"Tim," he said though, not quite there yet. None of us were. We were still at the curb, my hands at ten and two, my foot hard on the brake to make sure the cop would be watching me, not Dance, toeing the .22 out, nudging it towards the hole rusted in the floorboard. It was an old Indian trick: dump the incriminating evidence, circle back for it in a few hours. Or not. Either way there'd be no excuse to pull us in. The hole in the floorboard was why we drank cans—because a bottle makes noise on the asphalt. But a gun. It just flows down, matte black, invisible. Or it was supposed to.

It was already there, officer.

We don't know anything about it, officer.

Is it a crime to park on a loaded weapon?

But Dance started too early for any of our excuses, or too late, or I didn't have my seat reclined far enough to cover, or Don Ann made some motion with his hand, dragging the cop's eyes across the rear floorboard. Tim didn't do anything, though.

We'd rolled his window up in the grocery store parking lot when we were hiding the gun, but then pushed it back down as deep as we could; it was covered in him. He was in the door, on the back dash, under the vinyl, coloring the headliner. It was his car now. There was nothing Amos could do but open the door, catch him as he fell, cradle him like we couldn't, or weren't.

"She wasn't always gone," I told him—Sheri. "And even when she was, it wasn't all the way."

Amos looked over Tim's red chest at me and nodded, said he knew, he'd seen her too, walking near the walls of buildings, her hands in her pockets.

"Yeah?" I said, and then Dance started yelling—screaming—*no no no,* his saliva misting over the backseat, his orange leggings taking root, twining around his legs, keeping him there. He fought them, slapping the seat, the air, *Halloween*, and when we turned from him back to Amos and Tim, they weren't alone.

Standing naked with them was Tim's father.

Now Don Ann was shaking his head no, but that was just because he didn't understand. Like I did. Like Amos did. She was still out there.

Dance

Tonight. He was right, Lyndon: tonight. The end of October, the beginning of something else. Tim watching those three little Indians out the window, the cop's muzzle flash reaching nearly to the base of his skull. It singed his hair in half where it touched him and I collected it strand by strand, let it go out the window because it shouldn't have been him. He wasn't the one walking the fence lines for sheds the third month after Sheri left.

They were paying fifty dollars a pair at the gas station in town, more if you had a map of where you'd found them, the tines jutting up through the melting snow. Each time I thought there was going to be a deer there, shot through the gut, blasted, but there never was, just the sheds, worn smooth from the wind and the trees and the other bucks. Fifty dollars a pair. I was out before the rest of the reservation, my breath white even in my lungs. Junior passed on the road below, hauling hock wood, but didn't see me. Only the deer ever came up here. It was too steep. Even the highway to town curved around, switching back on itself, trading gas for transmissions.

I had the .22 with me then too, for grouse, but never heard any. Once there was a rabbit but it was too herky-jerky, like a point guard with his girlfriend watching, so I gave up. Where it had spun out though, the ground was different—blue, with white chevrons.

It was Sheri's ski jacket.

I held it and carried it and walked with it and finally filled its pockets with rocks, slung it as high into the canopy as I could.

She was gone.

I never told Lyndon, never told anybody, but then, God, when she rose up out of the sidewalk in her dress. The trees all came back—Spruce, Oak, Pine—and I had to look away until it was safe, until we were moving again, pulled over again, the red lights flashing behind us.

"Was it her?" I asked, but nobody answered. Lyndon was already in standard procedure mode—looking straight ahead, the car still in gear.

I went through the motions, my toe quiet on the .22, pulling it toward the void—Amos's trick, from when we were kids and the car had been his—but the trees were all around still, and there were sheds everywhere suddenly, and under the snow the deer, dead, walking up the sidewalk on the other side of the road from us.

"Was it her?" I asked again, Tim looking back to them in answer, and then came the undeniable sound of a stiff black holster creaking, a heavy gun like an index finger, pointing at the backseat.

It was so loud; it left a perfect hole in Lyndon's seatbelt, one in Tim instead of me.

I pulled the trigger of the .22 back against its guard four times, but it wasn't enough to stop any of this. The officer leaned against the car with one arm, his pistol clattering softly on the asphalt underneath us, and then he swayed back, into the papers.

"No." I said it myself, in answer. It wasn't her. It never was her. We pulled easy away from the curb, into November and all the months after November.

Discovering America

Because I'm Indian in Tallahassee Florida the girl behind the counter feels compelled to pull the leather strap ($1.19 per foot) around her neck, show me her medicine pouch, how authentic it is. "Yeah," I say, "hmm," and don't tell her about the one-act play I'm writing, about this Indian in the gift shop at the bottom of Carlsbad Caverns. His name isn't Curio but that's what the lady calls him when she sighs into line with her Germanic accent and her Karl May childhood. "You should do a rain dance or something," she tells him, she's never seen heat like this, like New Mexico. In the play she's sweating, he's sweating, and there's uncounted tons of rock above them, all this pressure.

In Tallahassee it rained all the time.

I stayed there for eleven months, nineteen days, and six hours.

Because I'm Indian at a party in Little Rock Arkansas, a group of students approaches me out of a back room of the house, ceremony still thick on their breath. In a shy voice their leader asks me what kind of animal my spirit helper is, and when I can't quite get enough tact into my mouth to answer, they make a show of respect, say they understand if I can't tell them, really. They tell me theirs, though: a grasshopper, a dragonfly, three wolves, and somewhere in there I become that tall, silent Indian in Thomas Pynchon's "Mortality and Mercy in Vienna," right before he goes cannibalistic in the middle of an otherwise happening party. The working title of the play I'm still writing is *The Time That Indian Started Killing Everybody*, and standing there with my beer I don't revise it.

In Little Rock there were all kinds of bugs I hadn't seen before.

I stayed there for five months, four days, and twenty-two hours.

Because I'm Indian in Odessa Texas the guy who picks me up off the side of the road asks me what kind. He's an oilfield worker. His dashboard is black with it. When I say *Blackfeet* he finishes for me with *Montana*, says yeah, he drilled up there for a while. Cold as hell. "Yeah," I say, thinking this is going to be an all right ride. He drives and tells me how when he was up there he used to ride a helicopter to the rig every morning, it was *that* cold. In trade I tell him how the National Guard had to airlift hay and supplies a couple of winters back. He nods as if this is all coming back to him, and then, with both arms draped over the wheel real casual, asks me if they still run over Indians up there? I turn to him and he explains the sport, even hangs a tire into the ditch to show me how it's done.

In Odessa the butane pumps go all night, and it's hard to sleep.

I stayed there for three months, fourteen days, and fourteen hours.

Because I'm Indian the guys at the warehouse in Clovis New Mexico add a single feather to the happy face that's been carved into the back of my locker ever since I got there. It's not like looking in a mirror. Every time it's not like looking in a mirror. My second week there we're sweeping rat droppings into huge piles, and when I lean over one to see what Butch is pointing at he slams his broom down, drives it all into my face. That weekend I start coughing it all up, become sure it's the hantavirus that's been killing Indians all over. My whole check goes into the pay phone, calling everyone, talking to them one last time, reading them my play, the part where Curio kills one of the gift-shop people the old way, which means he hits him across the face with a log of Copenhagen, then follows him down to finish it, out of mercy.

In Clovis they don't turn their trucks off so you can talk on the phone, so you have to scream.

I stayed there for four weeks, one day, and two and a half hours.

Because I'm Indian in Carlsbad New Mexico the crew I'm working with calls me Chief, motions me over every time there's another animal track in the dirt. "I don't know," I tell them about the tracks, even though I do, and for a couple of hours we work in silence, up one row, down another. Once I find strange and cartoonish tracks in my row—traced with the sharp corner of a hoe—but I pretend to miss them, pretend no one's watching me miss them. All this pretending. Towards the end of the day I pass one of the crew and, without looking up, he asks if I've scalped anybody today, Chief?

I unplant a weed from his row, look up for the briefest moment, long enough to say it: "Nobody you know." He doesn't laugh, and neither do I, and then later that night in a gas station I finish the play I started writing in Florida. It starts when the clerk wipes the sweat from his forehead, says how damn hot it is. And dry. I neither nod nor don't nod, just wait for him to say it.

In Carlsbad New Mexico the law is sluggish, slow to respond.

I stay there for sixteen hours, nine minutes, and fifty-two seconds, and when the rain comes it's not because I danced it up, but because I brought it with me.

Tom Buffalo Runner was our clown. Every morning at boarding school it was another thing—four pennies hammered into the space between Wally Little Plume's door and door frame, so he couldn't get out, had to go to geography without pancakes, or lemon juice in the wall-mounted shampoo dispenser, so that, with sunlight, one of us would be Custer blond, or a tampon he had stolen from the girls' dorm, left floating in the water of one of the toilets like a coup stick. But we got him back too, talking to him in algebra or poli sci while George Peters (Cheyenne) crawled under an impossible series of desks then passed Tom's textbooks back one by one, so we could untape the covers from them, turn the books upside down, then tape the covers back so that when Mr. Anderson or Lady Douglas found him sleeping head down on his desk, hiding under his hair, he couldn't pretend to be reading the book he'd been hiding behind. But sometimes we banded together too, sabotaging the sloppy joe mix in the cafeteria so that the principal had to burn a snow day, or soaping the fountain pink, or running various newbies' underwear up the flagpole, and one semester we even solved the mystery of the sea serpent in our local lake, built our own cardboard dragon head, then floated it out on a canoe, cornered the "original" sea serpent (our biology teacher Mr. Burroughs's "tourism project," as he called it), got our pictures in the paper. Great hunters. And then we went arm in arm back to our dorms, and the cafeteria tables were already swaybacked with food, the bank of pay phones ringing with our parents' well-wishes and concern, our mailboxes stuffed with cards, and our floor monitors, before lights out (what they thought was lights out), would lead us through some 49s, so that all we could think about was summer, dust in the headlights, but we could only get back there if we learned all our math, our science, our geography and history and literature, so we leaned as far over our desks as we could, helped each other with finals, fell in love with every girl from the East Wing at least once, but don't believe it. The way it really was was that they kidnapped us from our reservations and cut our hair off and burned it and cut our tongues out and used them for bait and called our parents savages and then scraped the religion off their walls and chewed it up and spit it into our mouths and told us it was enough, that we didn't need anything else. But then at night we collected in the dark corners they didn't know were there and told each other about this uncle we had, sneaking into America without a pass, running back ahead of forty or sixty or eighty horses, or our mother, what she gave the priest to eat that time he came to dinner, or a story we knew sort of, about this one man from the bow and arrow days, using ducks to get berries out of the water, or berries to get ducks, or making a man from a piece of flint, or a boy born from a clot of buffalo blood, a boy no jail made of wood or steel or words could ever hold, and then we crawled back to our beds and waited for it to happen like it always did when we told the stories right: one of us stumbling up from his sheets, falling to the plank floor then standing just as fast, feeling ahead of him for the windowsill, something to hold onto while his back humped over, his feet hardened into hooves, his eyebrows into black horns, the brown hair coating his body thick enough for any winter, his foreleg no longer useful on the windowsill, slipping off, the

hoof on the wood floor like a gunshot, calling our floor mon-
itor from his bed, to silhouette himself in the door just long
enough for the new buffalo by the window to see him, the
muscles of his hind legs already bunching, enough boy left in
him that he can still smile, enough boy left in us forty or sixty
or eighty years later that when the government comes in its
dark green cars to bring opportunity to the reservations, edu-
cation, we take our grandchildren under our arms and we run
through the trees like Indians used to

which is fast

Journal entry for group,
December 29, 1998

Acknowledgments

To my supercool agent, Kate Garrick: thanks for never not believing. To Brenda Mills: like it says, this one's yours. To Gerald Vizenor, for showing up on my voice mail one day: the message is still there. To Janet Burroway, for ushering a couple of these stories along: the rest probably wouldn't be there without them, without you. To Doug Crowell, for reading these all in record time, eleven years after reading my first story: Procol Harum's not in any of them, yeah? To my wife, for giving me the world: I like living in it with you. To my granddad, for all the rabbits we never shot: I think I understand. To turtles, which still terrify me: please stop. To Dekalb, which seems to be in a couple of these stories: thanks for all the herbicide. Don't know where else I could have inhaled it in such pure form. And, finally, to the receptionist the other day who smiled at me and said to someone in her phone, about the rain behind me, that it was because I was doing a dance, then clapped the necessary whoops from her mouth: thanks. That last story's for you.

Thanks to the original publishers of these stories:

"Venison": *Native American Writers 2000*, *South Dakota Review* 38, no. 1 (Spring 2000).

"Captivity Narrative 109": *South Carolina Review* 36, no. 2 (Spring 2004).

"To Run Without Falling": Pleiades 23, no. 2 (Spring 2003).

"Episode 43: Incest: *taint magazine* 2, no. 13 (March 2003).

"Nobody Knows This": *Bordersenses,* a bilingual Southwestern literary journal (vol. 6, 2003).

"Bile": *Open City* 14 (Winter 2001–2002).

"Filius Nervosus": Originally "Filius Nevosa" in *Gulf Coast* 14, no. 2 (Summer–Fall 2002).

"Last Success": *Cutbank* 48 (Fall 1997).

"Conquistadors": *Studies in American Indian Literature* 14, no. 4 (Winter 2002).

"These Are the Names I Know": originally "For Darius" in *Phoebe: A Journal of Literary Arts* 51 (Winter 1997).

"The Fear of Jumping": *Controlled Burn* 10 (Winter 2004).

"Carbon": *Blood & Aphorisms* 25 (Winter 1997).

"Every Night Was Halloween": *The Journal* 27, no. 2 (Autumn–Winter 2003).

"Discovering America": originally "The Scenic Wonders of America" in *Beloit Fiction Journal* 14 (Spring 2001).

To order or obtain more information on these or other University of Nebraska Press titles, visit www.nebraskapress.unl.edu.

CPSIA information can be obtained
at www.ICGtesting.com
Printed in the USA
LVOW12s1931261017
553890LV00003B/290/P